Ugly
Young
Thing

ALSO BY JENNIFER JAYNES

Never Smile at Strangers

Ugly Young Thing

JENNIFER JAYNES

Published by Thomas & Mercer, Seattle

www.apub.com

Amazon, the Amazon logo, and Thomas & Mercer are trademarks of Amazon.com, Inc., or its affiliates.

ISBN-13: 9781477827352
ISBN-10: 1477827358

Cover design by Cyanotype Book Architects
Library of Congress Control Number: 2014952002

Printed in the United States of America

For Mom.

Thank you for always being there for me.

PROLOGUE

URINE SKIDDED DOWN her leg, warming her bare skin. She was more terrified than she'd ever been, and in her short fifteen years, there had been plenty of reasons to be afraid.

A heavy downpour pummeled the small house, battering the living room window next to her. But Allie wasn't aware of the storm outside.

Only the storm inside the house mattered.

Her older brother was facing her, his eyes unfocused. In one hand he held a gun. In the other was the smooth stone he kept on his nightstand while he slept. The gun was pointed at her and he was rolling the stone around in the palm of his hand.

Hatred flashed in his eyes—and she could see just how much he'd come to loathe her.

"Please," she pleaded, tears flooding her eyes, making it difficult to see. "Please don't do this. I'll change. I will. I promise."

Please don't hurt me.

Thunder boomed outside, overpowering her words, so she wasn't sure if he even heard her. He just continued to stare, his eyes glassy. He swayed a little, and she wondered if he was on something, even though it wasn't like him to medicate with anything stronger than a beer or two.

The thunder died down and she tried again. "Just wait. You'll be so surprised at how nice I can be. How *normal.*"

"No," he said, his words slurring. "You'll *never* be normal."

"I will. I cross my heart. I . . . I love you."

His handsome face twisted. "Don't say that to me!"

"I'm serious. You're all . . . you're all I've got," she cried, holding her palms out to him, showing him how vulnerable she was, just in case he didn't already know. "You're all I've *ever* had. Mama was sick. I knew that. I hated her for what she did to you. For what she did to everyone, but *especially* you."

At that, he cocked his head. He seemed to weigh her words, trying to decide if, for once, she was telling the truth.

"I guess I just didn't know any other way to act," she added.

He stared at her for a long moment, then his face filled with rage. He shouted an expletive and sounded so angry Allie's face burned with shame.

But it was true. She *didn't* know how to act. At least not like others did. She didn't fit in like most others did. She was always the outsider.

Her brother had been her only friend, so when he started avoiding her, she lashed back. She said nasty things to him and told him he was a loser, although she didn't really think he was . . . and the more he ignored her, the nastier she became.

She was also frightened because he had grown sick, just like their mother had, and that summer he'd killed two teenage girls. The sheer fact that he'd done it really freaked her out. But what scared her even more was she feared he'd eventually get caught and be taken away from her.

Then what would she do?

How could she possibly live without him?

She didn't want him to be sent away. She loved him more than anything, but she was also deathly afraid of rejection. So, instead of saying "please love me again" or "I need you more than anything," she did and said hateful things. She wasn't really sure why she did what she did; all she knew was that she didn't know how not to.

Her brother's countenance shifted. The hatred and loathing in his eyes was now replaced with something different. Something that looked like pain. His face went fish-belly white, his expression blank.

Allie realized that the moment had come. She slowly backed away from him.

Please, no! Give me another chance, she wanted to yell, but her mouth wouldn't move.

The stone tumbled onto the living room carpet. The light draining from his eyes, he pressed the old army-issue .45 to his temple—and stared at her.

"Quit causing people pain," he said. "Just stop it. It's wrong." He blinked a few times. "And don't think this is about you, because it isn't. It's me. It always has been." With that, he inhaled sharply and his eyes flickered to the wall behind her. "God, please forgive me," he whispered.

And he pulled the trigger.

Allie clamped her hands against her mouth. "No!" she wailed. But, of course, it was too late.

"No, please. My God, no!"

Don't die! Don't leave me!

Her ears ringing, she went to him. Her older brother, the only person who had ever meant *anything* to her, was about to be gone forever. Just minutes before she was sure he was going to kill her, but in the end he had decided to kill himself.

He made a gurgling sound, his eyes now frozen on the popcorn finish of the ceiling, a flood of red spreading out beneath his head. His eyes fluttered once, then stayed at half-mast.

He went very still.

"No! NO! NO!" She fell to the carpet. Trembling, she lifted his shoulders and scooted her legs beneath his back so that his head lay on her lap. Ignoring the warm blood soaking her legs, she held on to his arm and sobbed.

Yes, he had murdered people. But he'd never hurt her. In fact, he'd taken excellent care of her over the years: protecting her from their psychotic mother, buying groceries, making sure she had most of the things she needed.

She studied his face, trying to burn a mental image of it into her mind so she would never forget what he looked like—and she noticed something different about him. The edges of his mouth were slightly upturned, as though he had been trying to smile. Like maybe, just maybe, he had finally found peace.

"I'm not as mean as I pretended to be," she whispered through her tears. "I've always loved you so much. I just wanted you to love me back and you . . . you wouldn't." She placed her brother's hands in hers and squeezed them tight.

Eyes clouded with tears, she realized she had to leave, and quick. Either go or risk becoming a ward of the state, and she couldn't let that happen. No one had ever controlled her or told her what to do—and she sure as hell wouldn't let anyone do it now, especially the government that her brother had hated so much. After all, if he hated it, *she* hated it.

Scooting away from his body, she ran to pack a bag. Three minutes later, just as she heard the first of the police sirens, she threw open the screen door at the back of the house and disappeared into the woods.

Thirty minutes after that, she was sitting, bloodstained and paralyzed with fear, in the passenger seat of an eighteen-wheeler.

She was headed west on Highway I-10, toward Texas.

CHAPTER 1

Nine Months Later . . .

HE STOOD OUTSIDE Sherwood Foods, a small supermarket in Truro, Louisiana, clutching a paper grocery bag as though he was waiting for someone.

And he was.

Just not in the sense that people might think.

The day was overcast and uncomfortably humid, but he persisted. Since he'd arrived thirty minutes before, there had been heavy foot traffic. Couples and families in and out. Hundreds of screaming, red-faced children.

Most people didn't seem to notice him. And the ones who did probably forgot about him two seconds after making eye contact. He wasn't especially memorable, which, of course, worked in his favor.

So far he hadn't bothered to smile at anyone.

No one had been worth a smile.

He'd managed to stop hunting for years, but like all addicts, it was always on his mind, somewhere, well concealed behind several layers of thoughts. Or, sometimes just barely cloaked, behind one or two. But the desire was always there. Fortunately, he'd managed to keep it in check.

Until now.

He thought about the headlines he'd read of the kid who had killed people in an adjacent town a year earlier and wondered if he and the kid had shared any of the same thoughts. He wondered if the kid felt vindication or remorse after the attacks or if he just went numb. In fact, he thought a lot about the kid. About how alike they might or might not have been. About how awful it was that he ended his life just as it was getting started. It disheartened him just thinking about it.

The newspapers reported the kid had always been a loner. That he'd had weight issues when he was younger. That maybe his desire to kill had been fueled by being bullied at a fragile age . . . which, of course, described *him* to a T. But who really knew exactly what drove people to the type of madness that made them kill? Was it nature or nurture? Or a combination of the two? Over the years he'd studied the topic relentlessly, but the more he studied, the more confused he became, so he'd decided to stop.

The itch was back. He barely slept, and the rare times he managed to, he woke up in a pool of sweat. And, as always, when he had the itch, the rage flooded in, sickening every cell of his body. The problem was that he only knew of one short-term cure for his itch: hunting. He first discovered this, almost by accident, at the age of sixteen.

When he hunted he abided by three rules: the prey had to be a woman, she had to be a certain type . . . and she had to smile at him. He had learned the hard way that men didn't satisfy his needs. Nor did just any woman. And the smile did two things: It gave the woman some control over her fate. It also provided more of a challenge, because most people didn't like to smile at strangers, which meant he often had to work for it.

The new life he was leading had him on edge. He'd been waiting around for months for something big that might not ever happen, something he wasn't sure about, and it made him tense. He needed the release.

His thoughts snapped back to the foot traffic. Just as long as SHE didn't find out, he'd be okay. So with HER, he'd been very careful. Out of self-preservation he'd learned how to lie very well to HER over the years. Still, something had changed. SHE was guarded now . . . not nearly as warm. They even argued—something they never did before. He sensed it was because SHE was still suspicious, and that disturbed him . . . and only made the itch worse.

He stared deep into the parking lot, his eyes narrowing as he watched a young, blonde woman step out of her white Honda Civic.

She was cute, but plain.

Not his type.

Plus, she didn't have that certain *attitude* he usually went for. That cool, confident, even arrogant one that usually meant trouble but also deeply attracted him. The type other women would call bitchy. The type who made his life miserable when he was a boy. He knew that this woman didn't fit that profile, so he dismissed her.

He shifted his attention to the next row of cars and he spotted a curvier, more fashionably dressed young woman who had just eased herself out of a Pathfinder. She was a brunette, and he could gauge her attitude in her presentation and movements alone.

His pulse quickened.

The woman's dark hair was sprayed stiff and she was wearing a sassy little shorts set, tall wedges, and oversized designer sunglasses. Her chin was tilted toward the sky, her spine straight as she fussed with her linen shorts, yanking them lower around her thighs.

Bingo.

But then the Pathfinder's back passenger door flew open and a young boy jumped out.

He frowned. No, too messy.

Loosening his grip on the grocery bag, he halfheartedly turned his attention back to the plain-Jane blonde as she approached the supermarket's automatic doors.

On closer inspection, he realized she was much prettier than he'd first thought. In that natural, girl-next-door sort of way. She appeared to be in her early twenties and had a thin, athletic build. Her blonde hair was long and pulled into a high ponytail.

As she drew closer, it was also more obvious that she was very self-conscious.

She would be so easy.

If only she were right.

It surprised him when, a few seconds later, his heart gave a little tug. He sensed something about her. Something special. He wasn't sure what it was, but now that she was closer, he could feel it.

Suddenly he was excited.

But . . . was she going to smile?

Please, let her smile, he thought, strangling his grocery bag. For the true test was always the smile. It was an important rule he kept because it gave them a little control. Made what he did to them a little more fair.

Made him feel a little more human.

If they smiled, they were meant for him. If they didn't, well, maybe they'd live long, happy lives. Maybe they'd become grandmothers. Great-grandmothers even. Happy ones.

If anyone's even capable of being happy anymore.

When he and she were not ten feet apart, she stumbled in her sandals.

"Whoa there," he said, his tone playful. He smiled at her.

8

She caught his eye and grinned sheepishly back, her face blooming into something truly beautiful. A light scar blemished her face, running the length of her forehead to her cheek, but it only added to her intrigue. "Guess I'm a little clumsy," she laughed.

His smile widened.

No . . . no, you're perfect.

CHAPTER 2

THE MOTOR IN the small air-conditioning unit sputtered, shattering the quiet of the motel room.

Allie stirred from her place beneath the heavy covers. She poked her head out and the frigid air chilled her cheek. Waking up in the morning was not one of her favorite things to do. It had become pointless, really. She was always exhausted, and her dreams were usually more pleasant than her reality.

Without fail, her first thought upon waking was always of her brother—and how desperately she missed him. Then, she would try to remember who was sleeping beside her.

It was usually a client.

Some lust-filled trucker who needed a warm body to sleep next to during long, lonely nights. Someone who had a loving woman waiting impatiently for him back at home.

Allie had followed in her mother's footsteps. She wasn't proud of it, but she didn't know how to do anything else, and it kept her alive. Plus, she desperately needed the company. Being alone scared her.

Yes, sleeping with men for money made her feel pathetic; disgusting even. But by now she was almost numb to it. She told herself that she was using *them*. Not the other way around. And as long as she managed to believe what she told herself, she was okay.

And yes, she was always someone's dirty secret. But at least now someone was paying attention to her. It was better than being the unwanted daughter of the local whore . . . or the loathsome sister her brother had always tried to get rid of. At least now people spent a little time with her. They even paid for it. Well, at least most did. She could count on two hands the number of times she'd been stiffed. Twice she'd even been knocked around. Just more experiences she had to shove to the back of her mind, because if she didn't, she would probably lose it.

With enough vodka in her, she was able to escape into a cloud of nothingness and feel confident and powerful. It was a much-needed, albeit short, escape until the alcohol's effects wore off and she discovered she was more used up than before and just as alone.

But her line of work ran in her family, so who was she to do anything different? After all, the apple rarely fell far from the tree. At least that's what her mother used to say.

She reluctantly pried an eye open. The motel room was pitch black. The thick drapes on the wide rectangular window of the room kept any and all sunlight at bay, so she had no idea what time it was. If it was morning, it was her sixteenth birthday.

Sweet sixteen.

Her muscles relaxed when she remembered she was with Johnny. He wasn't a client. He was her boyfriend. Well, maybe he wouldn't call himself that, but she liked to. He was from California, but he was driving a truck delivering baked goods from Texas to Oklahoma for the year to raise money for college tuition. They'd met late one night at a diner outside of Houston and had been together ever since.

She loved being close to Johnny. Loved curling up against his hard, warm body when they slept at night. Loved feeling his breath tickle her face as he slept. It lulled her so much it usually sent her

11

back to sleep for another hour, until he gently shook her awake so they could get back on the road. In fact, Johnny had been the only man aside from her brother who she'd ever even liked. She was hoping that he would save her.

She turned to face him.

And found his side of the bed empty.

Her bare feet hit the carpet. She peered around the corner to see if there was a light on in the section of the small bathroom that housed the toilet.

There wasn't.

His duffel bag? Her eyes darted to the corner where he always left it.

Crap! Gone, too.

His keys. He couldn't go anywhere without his keys. Were they still there?

She hurried to the little round table next to the window and saw that they were also gone. In their place was an unopened pack of Camel Lights, a twenty-dollar bill, and a note scrawled on the back of a guide to the motel's cable channels.

Li'l Bit,
It was real fun getting to know you.
  Now go home and do something with your life while you
still can.

  xoxo
  Johnny

"No!" Her shoulders slumped forward and she began to sob.

Johnny had been nice and handsome and funny. She could've grown to love him, even. Well, if she hadn't already. Maybe he could've been someone she could've grown old with. Someone she could've belonged to. Someone who could've taken good care of her.

She searched for the bottle of vodka that she always kept handy, but it was empty. Sighing, she drew the curtains and sunlight spilled into the room. Squinting out at the parking lot only confirmed his rig was gone. Tears rolled down her cheeks. Ripping open the cigarette pack, she shook out a cigarette and lit it, then took a long, desperate drag.

She had known it would only be a matter of time until Johnny would decide to leave her. She had been stupid to think he wouldn't.

Everyone abandoned her at some point.

Her father, when she was just two years old. Her mother, when she was twelve. Then her brother . . . and every other man she'd met over the past nine months since she'd been on the road.

She knew people considered her beautiful. Stunning, even. And it wasn't just something she'd made up. Everyone said it.

Such a pretty young thing, they'd always say.

People had seemed spellbound with her looks when she was a little girl. But when she turned twelve and started budding breasts, she noticed that her looks began to polarize people.

The stares she got from the men suddenly turned from innocent admiration to something that felt greedy . . . sometimes downright dirty. Women began to see her as a threat, their faces hardening just at the sight of her.

She didn't understand it because she thought she was far from pretty. Yes, since adolescence, she had learned to cover some of her flaws with makeup, and she was careful to hide most of her bad angles and avoid harsh lighting when possible. But still, it baffled her because when others looked at her, they seemed to see someone completely different than the girl who stared back at her in the mirror. The girl who, when she wasn't very careful, looked hopelessly grotesque.

Almost like a monster.

The relationship between her and her brother changed, too. He suddenly became aloof, distrusting, distant . . . and wanted nothing to do with her anymore. The harder she tried to be close to him, the more he resisted. And he'd been the only person she had ever truly cared about.

When she was younger he had taken good care of her and comforted her when she needed it. But then, things changed . . . and she'd somehow become the enemy.

She slumped lower in the tattered chair next to the window. Suddenly, she was as lonely and exhausted as she could ever remember being.

Without her brother and without Johnny, there was no point.

CHAPTER 3

THIRTY MINUTES LATER, Allie was still slumped over, smoking at the little table in the motel room. The sun was higher in the sky and people were emerging from their own ratty rooms. She watched enviously as families packed SUVs and minivans. Everyone seemed to be heading somewhere this morning.

Everyone but her.

She already missed Johnny. When she was with him, the big knots in her stomach loosened and she managed to pull more air into her lungs. Most nights he even held her in his strong arms. Something no one had *ever* done.

He had been the only one who had been truly nice to her for a longish period of time. And he'd been honest from the start. He'd said he wasn't in it for the long haul and one day would have to leave without her. He also said he could never take her home to his family.

And, of course, she knew why. She simply wasn't good enough.

She had done her best to keep Johnny. When he was around, she was always carefully made up, moisturized, and scented. She worked hard at strategically displaying her body, the only part of herself she was proud of.

She was also careful to always be situated to the right of him, so he could see the better side of her face, and she kept her chin pointing in all the right directions, so he didn't see her many bad angles.

Even while they slept, she wore a full face of dime-store makeup, so very careful not to expose her natural looks. Looks that often alarmed her. She was careful to present the image of someone she desperately wanted to be . . . an image that he must've finally seen through.

She'd also let down her guard lately, something she knew she shouldn't have done. It first happened one night while she was keeping Johnny company on his usual route, a run from Houston to Bridge Creek, Oklahoma. She was sitting in the passenger side of the rig sucking the jelly out of a donut and sipping a chilled Corona when she drunkenly admitted she was only fifteen. He spit out his Dr Pepper.

"So if you're from Louisiana and only fifteen, how the hell did you end up way out here?" he asked.

She shrugged. "I hitched rides."

"At fifteen? My mother barely let me out of her sight at fifteen. Besides, I didn't know shit back then."

Allie was beginning to think she didn't know shit either. Nine months before, she seemed to have more answers. Now, she was more than a little lost . . . and more desperate than ever.

"C'mon, things couldn't have been that bad at home," he prodded.

"Yeah, well, they were. Besides, there's no one left."

"What do you mean?"

She stared out the window. "It's a long story."

"Well, we're about a hundred miles from our next stop, so I'm pretty sure I have the time. Go ahead. Tell me."

Allie took a deep breath and then, stupidly, blurted it all out. She told him about her father abandoning the family. About her mother being a prostitute . . . and how she used to dump bodies in the pond behind Allie's childhood house. About how the woman had abused her brother and how screwed up he'd become. Then, about how her brother killed their mother and ended up taking care of Allie. How he paid the bills and bought the food but then became sick in the head and began hurting people, too.

"Nine months ago he killed himself, and now there's just me. That's what I mean when I say I'm all alone."

Allie's stomach knotted as she squeezed the last of the words out because as she was telling her story, she'd gotten the sense that she was doing something wrong. As though she were making a huge mistake telling Johnny the truth about where she'd come from. About who she was.

There's a reason you don't talk much, Allie. You just remember that, she reminded herself.

The two rode in silence. Allie stared down at the remains of the jelly donut on her hand and wished she could undo the last few minutes.

"And you're telling me no one is looking for you?"

Allie shrugged.

Johnny turned and stared at her, then his eyes went back to the road. For a moment, the silence was deafening. Then he started laughing.

Allie frowned, thoroughly confused. But after a few seconds, she got it. He thought she was joking.

"You have quite the imagination, Li'l Bit!" he said, then began laughing some more. "Oh my. Really, you're something else! C'mon, give me that beer. I think you've had too much!"

Allie found herself laughing, too—out of relief—because she realized that if he had believed her there was a good chance he wouldn't want her around anymore. That he wouldn't save her.

Now, sitting in front of the motel room window, she lit another cigarette and chastised herself. She should've known he was about to leave. After three weeks of traveling back and forth together on his pastry routes, out of nowhere two mornings ago he'd just said, "Go home, Allie. Surely someone misses you. Besides, you have no clue who I really am." His blue eyes had held hers as he said it. And it was the very first time she'd ever seen him look so serious.

But he was wrong. No one missed her.

Everything she'd said in the rig had been true. And she didn't care who he truly was. She would like him no matter what. After all, who was *she* to judge anyone?

After two hours and smoking all but three of the cigarettes, she finally rose. Her heart knocked angrily against her chest. The nicotine hadn't calmed her one bit. In fact, it seemed to have done the opposite.

Her situation was beyond hopeless and she was miles beyond exhausted. She had nothing and no one. The world was a frightening place. And a place where she had never seemed to belong. She was tired and just wanted it all to end.

She stuck her hand in her brother's backpack and rummaged around her belongings, drawing out a bottle of pills she'd stolen from a truck driver. She examined the label and wondered if there were enough of them to end it all—the whole miserable mess of her life.

She went to the room's little bathroom to fill up an empty beer bottle with water from the sink. Then she sat on the bed and took the pills two at a time—a total of twenty-three—until the bottle was empty.

The air conditioner kicked on, the fan sputtering. She walked back into the filthy bathroom and stared at herself in the mirror. Her gray eyes were puffy and raw. Black mascara coated her cheeks, and a thin stream of clear snot had worked its way out of a nostril.

No wonder no one loves you. You're hideous.

Drawing warm water into the tub, she undressed, stepped in, and lit another cigarette. Then she lay against the fiberglass and closed her eyes, welcoming the comfort of drifting away from her world. Away from the unbearable loneliness.

And hopefully toward her brother again.

CHAPTER 4

THE PRETTY BLONDE from the supermarket was in the master bathroom, running a bath.

He waited in the adjoining bedroom just inside the doorway, listening to her each and every movement. Hunting knife in hand, he stood motionless, enjoying the adrenaline rush. The heat coursing through his veins.

His short stint as a small-town local was making him claustrophobic. He was ready to be back in the big city. But he couldn't leave yet. No, he had to wait. He had responsibilities. People who finally needed to be taken care of.

She splashed quietly every now and then. But for the most part, she was quiet. She was reading a novel. He'd watched as she had taken it in with her. Some sort of thriller.

Apparently, she likes to be afraid.

A few minutes earlier, she'd walked from the bedroom into the bathroom, her firm little naked backside swaying left to right. She was holding a bottle of wine, a glass, and something else. Something odd.

A freshly sharpened knife.

Strange, he thought.

Eerie even.

In fact, during his first thirty minutes of being there, he'd watched her sharpen two knives in the kitchen. She'd placed one beneath her pillow before disappearing into the bathroom. The other was now in the bathroom with her.

He smiled to himself. *As if wielding a knife against someone like me will keep you safe.*

Maybe the knife had something to do with the thriller she was reading. Maybe the book had her just a little freaked out. Although he had watched her check the locks on all the doors and windows of the house, perhaps she was still feeling insecure. If she was, she had good reason to be. It had taken him less than a minute to pick the cheap lock on the back door.

Since he'd been in the house, he had learned several things about the woman. From the books strewn around her room to the affirmations scribbled on several sticky notes she had posted on various mirrors and walls, he could interpret her most private concerns.

She was having relationship troubles, or had at some point in her life.

She was seeking advice on getting out of debt.

And, she wanted to lose weight.

He thought her body was perfect. In fact, it looked much better naked than when it was in clothes. Luckily he'd been in eyeshot when she undressed and had been able to commit the image to memory. It was a memory he could replay over and over as much as he liked.

Wherever he liked.

She had small but perky breasts, a nice slender stomach, narrow hips, and strong, lean legs. Her behind was small, but high, taut, and plump in all the right places.

Splashes from the bathroom. She was moving around in there again. He tensed and another surge of adrenaline poured through him. When she became still again, his gaze went back to her things.

Her bed was unmade. She had tossed her panties, bra, and a pair of jeans on the floor. A T-shirt was also balled up on her bureau next to a dirty plate and a previously used wineglass.

She was a slob. She should be putting her efforts into keeping her space clean, not trying to lose weight. It put him on edge to see things in such disarray.

More splashes, these louder. She was getting out of the bath.

He smiled again and went to his hiding place.

CHAPTER 5

DUST SWIRLED IN the blistering air as the black Grand Cherokee sped away. Standing on the dirt drive, Allie lit a cigarette and stared at the small house . . . a place she hadn't seen in nine months. Since the night she'd watched her brother kill himself.

She inhaled a combination of smoke and putrid bayou air, then retched. Her eyes watered and the lining of her throat felt as though it had been scalded with acid. She had never felt so sick. It had been a whole day since she'd vomited the pills in the motel room and the pain hadn't eased a bit.

Back in the motel bathtub, the pills came back up, but after about five minutes of retching, she thought for sure she was still going to die.

Just not painlessly, like she had hoped.

Naked and shivering, she'd crawled out of the tub, across the dirty, threadbare carpet, and retreated back into bed, where she dry-heaved until she was kicked out of the room by the day manager, who had demanded thirty dollars for another day in order for her to stay. She would've given it to him, but all she had was the twenty-dollar bill that Johnny had given her, plus a little loose change.

She was such a loser.

She couldn't even manage to kill herself right.

Sick and dazed, Allie had stood, clinging to her stomach, outside the motel for what seemed an eternity before she was able to untangle her thoughts enough to figure out where she could go.

Just a place to rest until she didn't hurt so much.

Then slowly, it had hit her. The only place possible, really. The house in Grand Trespass, Louisiana, where she had lived with her brother. Her childhood house. The town that was little more than a pit stop for people who were going to *real* places, traveling the I-10 highway. It was a sad little place. And technically it wasn't even in Grand Trespass proper, but in Weston, an even smaller and drearier town.

It had taken Allie twenty-four hours and rides from four different men, but she'd gotten there. The problem was she was too afraid to go in.

She swallowed hard. Just seeing the house again made the reality of all that had happened there so much more real. She dragged on her cigarette and stared at a used hypodermic needle next to her foot.

The tall grass and wiry weeds had grown tall, strangling the old house. Old, faded strips of yellow police tape littered the sun-beaten front porch, and nasty graffiti in large red letters blared hateful things about her family against the peeling siding. Reading the words stung, and her knees grew so weak they came close to buckling.

Allie had been staring at the house for almost an hour when a searing pain shot through the center of her stomach, doubling her over and forcing her to finally go in.

It was now time. She *had* to lie down . . . to sleep.

Clutching her stomach, she shuffled up the dusty gravel path that led to the house and climbed the rickety porch steps.

She froze.

A skeleton of a dead cat—isolated tufts of coarse black fur still attached to its backside and tail—rested in the corner of one of the stairs. She wondered if it was the cat she'd been feeding during her last weeks in the house. The cat she'd heard her brother call "Ian."

Her eyes went to the front window. The glass was completely gone, leaving nothing but a dark, gaping hole into the living room. The front door was also ajar.

She opened the screen door, then pushed the wooden door wider, breathing in the musty odor of the neglected house. The scents of mold, decay, and urine flooded her nostrils. It looked like someone had taken a baseball bat to the room. Fragments of glass, drywall, stuffing, and pieces of furniture littered the floor. The couch slumped over with broken springs. Everything was coated in a thick layer of dust.

Her stomach lurched as her eyes locked on the bloodstained carpet. She stared at it for a long while, reliving that awful night. The one she still wanted so badly to do over.

She tore her gaze away from the spot where her brother had died and fumbled in her back pocket for another cigarette. As she took a lengthy drag, something cool slithered up her back. She spun around, clapping her free hand to the small of her spine, then the base of her neck, anxiously feeling for whatever it was. But nothing was there.

Then, she realized she felt cold. Very cold.

I just need to lie down, she told herself.

"Who's there?" a voice asked, coming from the kitchen.

Allie jumped. Stepping backward, she called out, "I live here. Who are you?"

Silence.

She grasped the metal knob of the front door. "Is someone there? Hello?"

Nothing.

She bent down and picked up a large shard of glass from the carpet and moved slowly through the living room, her pulse racing. "Hello?" she called again.

Silence.

A few minutes passed before she mustered the courage to tiptoe to the kitchen and peer around the corner.

An enormous hole had been dug in the center of the linoleum floor.

Probably where the cops had dug looking for more bodies. The rest of the floor was covered with litter: burger wrappers, discarded beer and soda cans, dirty paper towels, a pair of red panties, and a tennis shoe she didn't recognize. Litter was also strewn across the yellow Formica counters.

But there wasn't a soul in the room.

The screen door to the back porch was ajar.

Maybe the person got scared and bolted.

"Hello?" she called again, for good measure.

But her call was only met with more silence.

Her brother once told her that he thought that's how it all had begun with their mother. Although she'd suffered from depression for decades, one day, out of the blue, the woman just began hearing voices . . . *seeing things*. The doctor diagnosed her with a series of additional mental disorders, including paranoid schizophrenia, and her condition only worsened. That's when everything changed, he said, and the house became dangerous for everyone.

Not long after, their father left late one night for a six-pack of beer and never returned, which only made her mother's mind deteriorate faster.

Shortly after the conversation about their mother, her brother shut her out. Allie understood now that it was probably because he'd begun hearing the voices, too. And now *she*—

She shook the thought from her head and walked to the back door. Just as she was about to touch the knob, she stepped into a patch of cold air.

The hair on her arms stood on end.

She took three steps backward and the air was again warm and moist.

What the—*? No. I'm just so tired I'm hallucinating.*

Flicking her cigarette through a shattered window, she walked down the hallway to the small bedroom in the back of the house.

Her brother's bedroom.

CHAPTER 6

STREWN ACROSS HER brother's musty room was more litter from either squatters or idiot kids. And they'd had a real field day with the walls. This time Allie didn't subject herself to actually reading the graffiti.

Pieces of torn-up girlie magazines were everywhere. She knew those, though, had been her brother's work. He had been very weird when it came to pornography. She never fully understood his obsessive hate for it, but she knew it had something to do with their mother being the town prostitute. Also, probably the late-night visits their mother sometimes made to his bedroom.

His television and CD player had been busted. She pried open the little door that housed the CDs, expecting to find it empty, but it wasn't. She plucked out the unmarked disc that was in it and tucked it into her backpack. Then she climbed into the bed and pulled his musty army blanket on top of her.

She squeezed her eyes shut. She needed to sleep so that she could gain the energy to think again. To make sense of the big jumble of thoughts that pushed and pulled against her brain, threatening to rip it in two. But between the pain in her stomach and the ache in her heart . . . she couldn't.

She lay there, huddled, for hours, until the sun set and the moon took up residence in the sky. Until the tree frogs began their evening songs.

Then finished those songs.

She was pretty certain that all the other sixteen-year-olds in the area had been called home and fed, and were laying in safe beds by now. That she, Allie, was the exception.

There was no one left to care whether she was safe or not. In fact, no one had ever cared whether she was at home tucked safely into bed or running the streets, making it with truck drivers just so she could survive.

No one but her brother had ever cared whether she lived or died. And several months before he died, he'd stopped.

As she finally drifted off to sleep, her mind replayed a night when she was five or six years old. It was the first time she had seen her mother drag a man's body through the house. She still remembered the odor of death and the sickening bumping sounds the body had made as it slid from the carpet onto the linoleum, then out the back door.

It was just one of many times when she'd instinctively known to pretend she hadn't seen anything. But sometimes her mother would still come and have "the talk" with her. During those moments, it took everything she had to not reveal that she was afraid. To convince her mother that she wouldn't tell a soul.

Her mother had always been paranoid about the law, and rightfully so. But she and the sheriff had made a deal. He and his deputy would visit the house a couple of times a month in exchange for turning a blind eye to her career path. But when it came to the murders, she eluded them altogether. She was a very beautiful and intelligent woman. She was also incredibly crafty.

During the scariest of nights, Allie crawled into bed with her brother and together the two had listened to the savagery that happened within the house's walls. Lying so close to him, she could feel his heart hammering inside his chest. Somehow knowing that they were going through it together helped make it easier to survive. Allie had been relieved when he finally killed their mother—and some of the madness stopped.

Since she was a little girl, all Allie ever wished for was the chance to live a normal life. To not be afraid all the time. To be normal. To be wanted and loved. But all of the pain had taken its toll on her, and now she only wished for a quick, painless escape from it all.

Whether she deserved it or not.

———

The memory of being attacked by a trucker hours earlier—the third of the four men who'd helped Allie get back to Louisiana —resurfaced that night in Allie's nightmares.

"You look awful exhausted," the trucker said, his cheeks rosy, his eyes kind. "Why don't you crawl into my sleeper compartment and get a little shut-eye while I drive?"

Her stomach was killing her, so it had seemed like a no-brainer. But seconds after she crawled back into the cluttered area, he crawled in behind her.

She kicked and screamed as his lips ground against her face and his big, calloused hands roamed up the legs of her shorts.

"Get the hell off me!" she screamed. But he wouldn't. Instead, he clamped a big hand over her mouth.

"You know you want it." He grinned. "If you didn't, you wouldn't be wearin' those sexy little booty shorts. Isn't that what they call them nowadays?"

She managed to pull his hand away. "Get off me, you old perv!"

The word seemed to hit a nerve. He stopped and stared into her eyes. "I'm not a pervert," he said, his eyes flashing.

"Help!" she shrieked. "Someone help me!" Someone would hear her. Someone would have to hear—

The man gripped her shoulders and shook her, knocking the air from her lungs. He threw her to the mattress and clamped his hand against her mouth again. "Yell again and I'll kill you. We clear on that?"

She nodded.

He pinned her down and kicked open her legs. She lay still, knowing it wasn't only futile to keep fighting, it was dangerous. Maybe if she let him have his way, he wouldn't be angry afterward and would just let her go.

She squeezed her eyes shut and made herself go limp, breathing in sour sweat and motor oil. Choking back a sob, she forced her mind to wander to some distant place. She swore to herself that if she made it out alive, she would never, ever sleep with a man again, especially for money. She'd had enough: the constant disgust she felt for herself, the attacks, the flat-out ugliness of it all.

Suddenly someone rapped loudly on the cab's window.

The man's eyes widened. Apparently her screams had been heard.

Cursing, the man rolled off her. She clawed her way into the front seat, then opened the door and lowered herself out of the rig. Squinting against the blaring sun, she realized several people had been drawn by her screams. Other truck drivers, random gas station customers. A woman clutching a screaming little boy. They all stood several feet from the truck, staring.

The man who had knocked on the door reached out a hand to help her to the pavement, but she dodged his touch.

A floorboard in the small bedroom creaked, drawing her from the dream. Beneath the blanket, her eyes sprang open.

Where am I? she wondered, her mind scrambling to get her bearings. Then she remembered. She was at her childhood house. In her brother's bedroom.

And . . . she had heard something. Or else it had been the dream. *Yes, probably the dream.*

But she had to be sure. Reluctantly, she pushed the blanket away from her face.

A figure was looming over her.

Her heart caught in her chest and she screamed.

CHAPTER 7

ALLIE SAT, SLUMPED, in the passenger side of the Camry with her eyes squeezed shut. The portly caseworker from the Department of Children and Family Services was navigating the twisting, country roads at a terrifying speed.

The windows were down and Allie's long, dark hair whipped around her face, stinging her cheeks. She pulled at the cotton shirt that was plastered to her skin with sweat. It was so hot and humid that her sweat even seemed to be sweating.

"You okay?" the caseworker asked.

"I'd be more okay if you'd just slow down," Allie muttered, her eyes still clamped tight. "You drive like an idiot."

"Oh heck, I could drive these roads blindfolded," the woman said and continued to speed. "Sorry about the heat. My AC crapped out a couple of hours ago."

The woman told Allie that she'd gotten very lucky. That an old woman—the "Cadillac" of foster mothers, she'd called her—was going to take her in and foster her until they could find her a "forever home."

Obviously, the woman didn't know her, because Allie had never been lucky. Good luck wasn't a luxury that was in reach of girls like her.

They'd driven for ten minutes or so when the woman finally pumped the brakes and brought the car to a steady crawl. Allie opened her eyes and watched as they turned onto a smooth concrete drive that led to a sprawling ranch-style house painted a pale yellow with blue trim. The lawn was greener than any lawn she'd ever seen. It was so perfect-looking it almost looked fake.

She sunk even further into the worn vinyl seat and closed her eyes again. She knew that the second the car stopped, she should run . . . but she knew she wouldn't. She had no fight left in her. She was hollow and weak, and all she wanted to do was curl up somewhere and sleep. She couldn't care less what happened to her anymore.

She hadn't cared when the deputies removed her from her childhood house. She hadn't cared in the emergency room when they poked and prodded her and the town sheriff asked her an insane number of stupid questions about her brother and the murders. She didn't care that she was supposedly getting a foster mother. She just didn't care. None of it even seemed real, so why should she? All she cared about was closing her eyes for a very long time.

The car shuddered as the engine cut off. "Here we are!" the woman practically shouted. "Try not to screw this up. Some of these homes are downright scary. And let me tell you, Miss Bitty is as good as it gets. Caring, nurturing, generous. She's God's gift to foster kids. Like I said, you really lucked out."

Allie opened her eyes. She gazed at the plush, well-manicured bushes that lined the front of the house, the purple hydrangeas and blood-red roses in little friendly-looking painted planter boxes that hung from the whitewashed porch.

A man pushed a lawn mower along the side of the house, while another carried a toolbox and some fencing to the backyard. Still another was sitting in a rocking chair on the far side of the wraparound porch, reading a newspaper.

The caseworker got out of the car and shouted a quick hello. Then she bent over and poked her head back into the car. "C'mon, Allie. Put on your best face and let's go. Don't make this more difficult than it has to be."

Waiting on the porch was an old lady with long gray hair piled on top of her head. She was barefoot and wore a sleeveless top and white cotton pants. She looked harmless—certainly not the type who ate homeless teens—although Allie knew better than to stake much on appearances.

Allie mustered all her energy to drag herself out of the car.

"Well, c'mon," the old woman prodded, smiling. She motioned for Allie to come up on the porch. "What are you waiting for?"

On leaden feet, Allie climbed the steps, taking in the clean scent of freshly mown grass. She wondered what the old woman knew about her. What the file contained that the caseworker was carrying. More importantly, why the woman would even take her in after learning about her past—because surely the people at the agency had told her all about it.

"Here she is, Miss Bitty," the caseworker said. "This is Allie."

The old woman leaned forward to get a closer look. "Poor dear, what happened to your face?"

Allie stared down at the porch, sweat beading on her brow.

"She was attacked while hitchhiking," the caseworker said. "She won't say much about it, though. Just getting that much was pulling teeth."

The old woman frowned. "My word."

"Well, like I mentioned on the phone, if at any point you find that she's too difficult to handle—"

Bitty silenced the woman with a wave of her slight hand.

"It's just that I'm afraid she's going to be, um, a little more *difficult* than the others," the caseworker said. "She isn't too happy about being here. And she has quite the mouth on her."

"Is that right," Miss Bitty said. More of a statement than a question. Allie could feel the woman's bright eyes boring into her. "Well, I'm always up for a good challenge, so I think we'll get along just fine."

Allie gazed past the woman and said nothing.

"Cat got your tongue, girlie? You can talk, can't you?"

Allie bristled and reached for something nasty to say, but instead, a wave of bile flooded her throat. "Yes," she managed weakly.

"I'm impressed," the old woman said with a smile.

"That makes one of us," Allie muttered, managing to hold her gaze. The old woman seemed to want to be playful, but Allie wasn't in the mood.

"Allie!" the caseworker gasped.

The old woman's smile broadened. "A little spitfire, I see."

A pain shot through Allie's raw stomach. Wincing, she clutched it, keeping her eyes locked on the porch.

Please, lady, I just want to sleep. Please, let me sleep.

The old woman frowned. "Something wrong with your stomach?"

"We just came from the emergency room. She tried to overdose on some pills," the caseworker said. "I have her medications from the hospital."

Bitty nodded.

"She also has a more in-depth physical scheduled . . . and the sheriff's department wants to interview her again. I have all the information written down for you. Dates, times. Of course I'll have to be present during any questioning of a minor, so if anything changes, I'll need to be notified."

The old woman nodded her understanding, then held out a sun-withered hand to Allie. "I'm Bitty. It's wonderful to meet you."

Allie glanced at Bitty's hand but didn't take it.

"Allie?" the caseworker prompted.

Bitty pulled her hand back and placed it on a petite hip. "I hear that you've had a pretty traumatic year, Allie. I'm sorry about your loss."

"It's none of your business," Allie said. She wanted the words to sting, but they sounded weak. So weak Allie could barely hear them leave her mouth.

"Allie," the caseworker warned.

"No, it's okay. She's come to the perfect place," the old woman said and led them into the house.

Once inside the air-conditioned foyer, she turned to Allie. "Let's give you the two-minute tour, then let you get some sleep. You look like hell."

CHAPTER 8

TWENTY MINUTES LATER the caseworker was gone and Allie was alone in a bedroom that matched the exterior of the house. She sucked in the air-conditioned air, grateful to finally get some relief from the oppressive heat, and scanned her surroundings.

Next to one of the room's two windows was a rocking chair. A big brown teddy bear sat in the middle of it, smiling dumbly at her.

She shot it a dirty look.

There was no way she was going to trust this new situation. The old woman. The nice house.

Several plants and a large bowl of sunflowers topped a bureau, along with a CD player. Allie set her backpack on the bed and fumbled for the CD that she'd found in her brother's room. She walked across the room and stuck it in the music player.

A moment later Bob Dylan began crooning his sorrowful song, "Lay, Lady, Lay."

Allie squeezed her eyes shut and listened. Her brother had played that very song over and over the last month of his life, as though he'd become obsessed with it.

Oh God, I miss you so much.

Why did I have to screw up so badly?

After the song ended, Allie opened her eyes again and gazed at the room. The old lady had said that the bedroom was hers. But obviously the woman didn't know Allie, because Allie would never deserve something so nice.

She was a nobody.

Even worse than a nobody, she was trash.

And once the lady discovered she was, everything would vanish: the room, the hospitality. The big warm welcome into the old woman's home.

Never trust a good thing. It was something her mother had preached on a daily basis—and the sentiment had stuck.

Across from the bed was a door. Opening it, she was surprised to find a private bathroom. She flipped on the light and stepped inside. Everything was so shiny and spotless it practically gleamed.

She caught her reflection in the mirror and her hand went to her cheek. The truck driver had really done a number on her. The right side of her face was bruised and an angry cut extended from her left ear to her nose.

"Crap," she muttered, grazing it with a finger. She caught sight of the rest of her face and shuddered.

Gross.

Quickly turning from the mirror, she tried to recount everything that had happened since returning to Louisiana: the sheriff's deputy ordering her from her brother's room in the middle of the night and shuttling her to the hospital, the sheriff questioning her about her brother and the murders, then arriving at the old woman's house.

She could only remember snippets of all the events. Other than that, it was all one big blur.

Back in the bedroom, Allie went to the bedside table. Miss Bitty had prepared a large mug of soup and left it there before leaving her alone to settle in. A small plate of dark crackers and a few pills sat next to it. Allie quickly downed the food. It was the first time she had eaten anything decent for as long as she could remember. Hell, it was the first time she'd eaten *anything* for as long as she could remember.

Returning the empty dishes to the bedside table, Allie decided to take the pills, hoping they'd help with the pain. After downing them, her eyes found the window. She felt certain she knew where she was and it wasn't very far from her childhood house. Maybe only a mile, give or take, if she cut through the center of the woods.

Once she had a chance to rest and get her head straight, that's exactly where she'd go. They couldn't keep her here against her will, no matter how old she was. Once she felt well again, she'd fight them tooth and nail and they'd want to forget all about her. They would be sorry they'd even known her name.

Kicking off her flip-flops and shrugging off her shorts, she peeled the comforter and top sheet back and crawled in. The bedding smelled sweet and fresh, like the magnolias that used to bloom outside her childhood house. The scent relaxed her. She'd never experienced anything so nice. So clean.

Don't you dare get used to this, she told herself.

Don't you freakin' dare.

Then she closed her eyes and plunged into a deep, dark sleep.

CHAPTER 9

HE HAD SPENT most of the afternoon in the young blonde's house, rummaging through her things. Lying on her bed. Trying to only think about her and not the beautiful teenage girl who had just arrived in town.

As he waited, he even did her dishes.

But the dishes hadn't been planned.

By 3:00 p.m., he'd grown so disgusted he decided to do the dishes for her. It had begun as just simply washing one dish. Drying it. Putting it away. Then he stared at the others—all crusted with filth—and decided to do just one more.

When he couldn't stand it anymore, he dropped the stopper into the drain, filled one side of the sink with soapy water, and scraped and cleaned the rest. Then, when they were dry, he put them away in their respective cabinets and tucked the clean silverware into a drawer.

He hoped he would get a glimpse of her face when she noticed his work. *What will run through her mind?* he wondered.

He'd learned more about her during the visit. Her name was Hope Smith. She was twenty-four years old and worked as a waitress at a local diner. She had been born and raised in Southern California, and was an only child, newly single, and taking college classes online. The house was her great-aunt Ester's. Apparently Aunt Ester had just been placed in an old folks' home outside of town due to Alzheimer's.

Aunt Ester's Cape Cod was less than a decade old and on an acre of land. It was pretty sturdy for newer construction but sickeningly easy to get into.

If only people knew how easy it was to enter their homes they would surely have difficulty sleeping at night. If people knew half the things going on around them, they'd be petrified.

Like most houses, there weren't many good places to hide. He'd found a closet with a water heater in the kitchen that was decent. The door had vented slats and an acceptable vantage point of her cluttered breakfast nook. Then there was her bedroom closet, which had the same vented slats, but the vantage point was practically useless unless Hope was standing directly in front of her bureau.

His favorite, though, was the four-poster bed that rested on plastic lifts. That had been a wonderful find. It was spacious enough that a baby water buffalo could probably lay beneath it, and there was a filmy skirt that skimmed the floor, which helped to further veil his presence.

His favorite hiding spot had always been beneath the womens' beds.

Mostly, though, he'd been limited to hiding just around a corner from where she was. Shadowing her . . . moving along with her as she moved through rooms. He had to be light on his feet, which was sometimes difficult, but doable. After all, he'd had years of practice. It excited him to know he could be discovered at any time. The thought of it made gooseflesh rise on his arms.

Whenever possible he liked to delay his gratification by spending time with them before the main event. He watched their movements, discovered their complexities, learned their scent before it was laced with fear. It made what he was about to do to them even more exciting. Usually he spent several hours. Maybe a day or two.

But Hope was proving to be different. With anyone else, he would've already made his move. But, unlike the others, just being near her soothed the itch, made him feel better. More alive. The air was electric when she was around.

He wasn't sure what it was about her, because on the surface she was all wrong. She was nothing like the others. His gut had picked Hope. Not his head.

He would wait to perform his big reveal until she discovered him.

He continued to count down the minutes until she'd be home. Thankfully her patterns the last few days had been like clockwork. Her schedule for the week was stuck to the refrigerator with a magnet shaped like a smiley face.

Most evenings, she brought home a Styrofoam container of food, grabbed some wine and a knife (or two), went upstairs, cleaned up in the bathtub or sink, and then crawled into bed.

She also would leave the dirty Styrofoam container on her bedside table overnight and wouldn't bother to pick it up well into the next day. He grimaced as he imagined the roaches that it could attract.

He had an intense fear of the filthy insects. They were one of only three things that he'd ever feared. The other two were being trapped indoors . . . and abandonment.

Just thinking about any of those fears made his gut twist.

———

"No, seriously. my dishes were, like, done," Hope told someone on the other end of the line.

Pause.

"No, I'm not shitting you. They were done and I didn't do them. Trust me, I'd remember."

A longer pause. Her tone went from incredulous to defensive.

"No, I *haven't* been drinking."

He listened from beneath her bed as she lied to her friend. He had just watched her pour a glass of red wine and down it in three gulps before pouring a second glass and picking up the phone.

"Look, I'm just saying. Someone did my dishes and I'm, like, incredibly creeped out. I mean, who would do that? And no one but my aunt's lawyer and me even have copies of the house keys."

Pause.

"And tell them what? That someone broke into Aunt Ester's house and did my dishes? Seriously. Look, forget it. I'm tired. I'm going to bed."

She hung up the phone and took a seat on the bed.

The mattress squeaked angrily above him.

She pulled off a pair of black tennis shoes. A moment later, they whizzed across the room, hitting the closet door.

Every nerve ending in his body was aroused by being so close. If he were to reach out, he could easily seize one of her slender ankles.

"Like I could really forget cleaning that whole damn kitchen," she muttered to herself. "I need new friends. Mine are *complete* dumbasses."

More wine splashed into the glass, then her legs disappeared.

The mattress squeaked several times as she got comfortable. The television clicked on and she channel surfed, eventually settling on a reality show he was familiar with. Every once in a while he heard her chuckle.

She had a beautiful laugh.

After several minutes she switched the television off. Then he heard a click as she switched off her bedside lamp, bathing the room in darkness.

He squeezed his eyes shut and listened, lulled by the woman's presence. When he heard quiet snores, he slipped out from beneath the bed. His heart hammering in his chest, he stared down at her and breathed in her scent mingled with the red wine.

He savored having so much power. Being the one who ultimately decided the woman's fate. The whens, the whats, the hows. As a child he was powerless.

But he was far from powerless now . . . and he was still making up for lost time.

The muscles in his left cheek jumped. "Good-bye, Hope," he whispered. "I'll be back for you."

He left the room and headed home.

CHAPTER 10

"TIME TO GET UP," Miss Bitty said, her tone firm. "And don't give me any lip, young lady. Solitude can be good, but too much is damaging. I've been around long enough to know."

Allie lay buried under the covers, curled into a sweaty ball. She knew she'd been in bed for three or four days, but she was still tired. Since she'd been at the old woman's house, she had only opened her eyes for a few minutes at a time, for food and to use the bathroom.

Every time she surfaced, there was a new dish on her bedside table. Fragrant soups with green stuff floating in clear broth, sour breads and herbed crackers, big colorful salads, chopped vegetables with bowls of dip, pitchers of water, mugs of tea . . . and sometimes, pills.

When she ate, she often heard voices down the hall, or the drone of a television set. A pan scraping against a stove top. The clatter of dishes being stacked in cabinets.

Sometimes while she slept, she heard footsteps in the doorway, the old lady slinking into the room, setting down food and watching her a bit before leaving. But whether Allie was aware of it or not, new food was always waiting when she woke.

"Allie? It's time to get up, girlie."

The old bat was still standing next to the bed.

Allie winced from beneath the covers, her head pounding. It felt like someone had kicked her in the skull while she slept.

What did the old woman want from her? Surely to put her to work. That *was* what foster parents were notorious for, right? Sitting on couches, eating bonbons, watching Jerry Springer while rent-a-kids mopped their floors and washed the windows?

"Did you even read my file?" Allie asked from beneath the covers.

"Yes, I did."

"Then why the hell am I here?"

A slight pause. "I don't understand."

Allie didn't respond.

"You can't stay under there forever. Besides, you have two appointments today. You have to meet your therapist, then I have to take you back to the doctor."

Therapist?

Her caseworker had mentioned she would need to see one. But, as far as Allie knew, only rich people saw therapists.

Maybe it was a ploy to get more information from her about her mother and brother. The sheriff had been awfully curious when he questioned her at the hospital.

Allie found it almost insulting that so many people were suddenly interested in her. Now that they realized she was the daughter and sister of murderers, she was finally worth their time. Where had everyone been all those years when she and her brother were suffering at the hands of their mother? Were they not worth saving back then? Did it really take people dying for her to finally be worth saving? It made no sense.

"How's your stomach?"

Allie's hands went to her middle, and she was surprised to realize the rawness had subsided. "Fine."

"Good. Then, after your appointments, I'm taking you shopping."

Shopping? "What kind of shopping?"

"We're buying you some decent clothes to wear."

Allie frowned from beneath the covers. No one had ever taken her clothes shopping.

Was this some sort of trick?

Still, she emerged from the covers, blinking against the morning sunlight filtering in through the window.

"C'mon now. I don't have all day. We have a lot of territory to cover," the lady said, a metal watering can in her hand. She shot Allie a quick once-over and frowned. "And a lot of work to do on you."

Allie had always wondered what it would be like to own new clothes. Instead, once or twice a year, her mother would come home with black lawn bags filled with clothes from the Salvation Army. They were always full of faded hand-me-downs that never fit quite right.

"I need you looking presentable if you're going to live here with me," the woman said. "You're showing way too much skin for sixteen."

"Says you. I like how I dress."

"Well, you shouldn't, so get up. You've been in bed for three days. I need you in the kitchen in an hour."

Allie wasn't sure how to feel about the old woman barking orders. She'd never had anyone tell her what to do or care what she did. She would have expected to be furious, but for some reason she wasn't. She was only curious.

When she was younger, it wasn't out of the ordinary to go several days without even seeing her mother. Allie would hang around the house, hoping to tag along with her brother as he went on with his days. On those rare occasions when she did get stuck at home with her mother, Allie would hole up quietly in her bedroom as strange men came and went, or she would walk the woods alone with one of her brother's books in hand.

He'd had so many.

Toward the end of his life most of them had been true crime: books on Ted Bundy, Jeffrey Dahmer, the Hillside Strangler, and more. It seemed as though he had some sick fascination with the way their minds worked. Either that or he was just trying to understand his own. Unlike her brother or mother, Allie had never had the desire to kill, and she hoped to God that she never would.

Allie studied Miss Bitty as she walked around the room watering the plants. She wasn't wearing a stitch of makeup, but she was still very beautiful for her age. Her thick gray hair was piled messily in a mound on top of her head, but it looked nice on her. Fitting. Her skin was smooth and her green eyes were bright and intense.

Her beauty is effortless. It's so unfair.

Allie felt a twinge of jealousy. If only she could look that good without all her war paint, without all the effort and strategies, life would be much, much easier.

From what she'd witnessed so far—the clean, comfortable house, the good food, the confident way the woman carried herself—Miss Bitty really had her shit together. Allie had never met a woman like her before. She found her fascinating.

With a start, Allie realized that Miss Bitty was finished with the plants and was now staring back at her, her old, bright eyes twinkling. Most people found it insulting to be scrutinized so openly; this woman obviously didn't. Allie narrowed her eyes. "I'll go with you, but don't think for a second that I trust you."

The lady didn't bat an eyelash. She actually looked amused. It made Allie uncomfortable, so she shot the old woman one of her fiercest looks.

"Be in the kitchen in one hour," Miss Bitty repeated, and left the room.

CHAPTER 11

MISS BITTY STOOD at the center island of the kitchen, trying to shove certain memories to the back of her mind.

She kept many horrible secrets. Secrets that ate away at her on a daily basis. Secrets that had eventually forced her to assume a new identity and become a new person entirely.

In the early '90s, her life took a devastating turn—and for a while she lost faith in God. She also lost all faith in herself and her values.

But a decade later she decided to turn her life around. She switched careers and became a wellness coach. She made sure that her home environment was in alignment with her health goals. She ate only high-nutrient foods to nourish her body and she was mindful about only thinking positive thoughts . . . although the negative had an insidious way of creeping in.

She practiced meditation, yoga, and energy work and was nothing but positive and helpful when interacting with others. She'd also been caring for foster children for almost sixteen years.

It was part of her repentance for all the devastation she'd once caused—and the only way she could manage to sleep at night.

Now she had three big projects to focus on. Three special callings. One of which, a little less than a year ago, required her to pack up her business and personal life and move from Southern California, where she was born and raised, to southern Louisiana: a place where people were far more likely to own an AR-15 assault rifle than a high-powered blender.

Her colleagues thought she'd lost her mind, but she'd managed to keep over 80 percent of her clients via phone sessions. On top of that, within months she found herself also overwhelmed with local clients through word of mouth alone. People were dealing with health issues everywhere, *especially* in places like Louisiana.

Now she stood in front of the big island in her kitchen, slicing a pineapple. Her newest traveling client was reading something on an iPad at the kitchen table.

She studied him.

Joe Hicks was a middle-aged, overweight businessman from Southern California. They'd known each other in California for years, so it hadn't really surprised her when he called and asked for her help. He'd been in need of it for a long while. He just hadn't known.

Miss Bitty wasn't a personal fan of the man. He was known for shady business dealings in the California area and had been ostracized by much of the entertainment community, but she'd decided to take him on as a client anyway. Everyone deserved help, especially people who seemed as lost as he was.

Joe was going to be a tough client. She had already noticed that he liked to hide contraband in his room: cigarettes, candy bars, and soda pop. He was a sneaky one, that Joe.

But that was okay . . . she was sneakier.

She'd make sure that when they began detox, most of those things would be gone.

Joe was going to be living in the guesthouse for a minimum of six months. Months that would be somewhat long and hard for him—at least in the beginning—but Bitty knew he'd be thrilled with the outcome. The experience would be life changing. It always was with her neediest clients.

Bitty felt the energy in the room shift. Knife in midair, she looked up and saw Allie in the doorway, her gray eyes flashing in defiance.

The old woman examined the girl, head to toe, taking in the face full of caked-on makeup, heavy black eyeliner, and loud red lipstick. She wore the same faded blue half-shirt, scraggly, cutoff denim shorts, and flip-flops she'd arrived in. Slung over her shoulder was the military green backpack she'd slept with since her first evening. Bitty guessed it contained all she had left of her previous life.

Despite the tacky way she presented herself, the girl's beauty was undeniable. It was easy to see how it could attract trouble. Bitty would have to keep a sharp eye on all of her male clients, even the hired help, because she knew from experience that no matter how well you thought you knew people, you really didn't know them at all. Or what they were capable of.

She hated pessimistic thoughts, but it was reality, and she had lived it and learned the hard way.

"I laid a shirt out for you to wear today," Bitty said, her eyes grazing the girl's taut abdomen. "Did you see it?"

"Yeah."

"Then why didn't you put it on?"

"Why should I?"

"To cover your skin."

The girl's eyes hardened. "I happen to like my skin."

"That's fine, but before I take you anywhere, you will change. And that's that."

Allie didn't say anything.

"Well, don't just stand there like an old bump on a log. Have a seat and eat your breakfast."

Bitty continued to study the girl as she walked to the table. Yes, physically, the girl was gorgeous. Almost shockingly so. Her skin was tanned and smooth, her dark hair long and silky. She had lean limbs and curves in all the right places, and her big gray eyes were nothing short of breathtaking.

It hadn't been included in the caseworker's file, but Bitty guessed that Allie had been some type of sex worker. It wasn't just the clothes and makeup, but also a certain guarded quality in her eyes. Girls like her usually related to men much more easily than to other females, so Bitty would make sure she had access to a man she could talk to. Someone outside of the buttoned-up confines of a therapist's office.

Miss Bitty had the perfect man in mind. Allie was definitely going to be a challenge, but that was okay. Miss Bitty liked challenges. She would fix the girl because that's what Bitty did.

She fixed people because she didn't know how to fix herself.

CHAPTER 12

ALLIE STOOD AT the kitchen table, wringing her hands. An overweight man sat across from her, entranced by his iPad. As he reached for his coffee, he glanced up and noticed her.

Startled, he leapt up, a beefy thigh clumsily bumping into the chair next to him. Chair legs scraped against the tile floor.

His face exploded into a smile and he extended a big hand. "Oh, hi there. Great to meet you," he said. "Joe. Joe Hicks." The man's face was mottled and puffy, and his belly spilled over khaki pants. He looked a little too pleased to see her.

Just like every other man she'd ever met.

She refused to give him her hand, the memory of the truck driver still weighing heavily in her mind. She didn't trust men. In fact, she didn't trust anybody.

The man's round cheeks reddened. He withdrew his hand and sat back down.

Bitty appeared at the table. "Allie, where are your manners?"

Allie didn't answer. Since leaving the bedroom, her pulse seemed to have tripled and she was having a difficult time catching her breath.

The old woman went on. "Joe, this is Allie. She's the new foster child I told you about."

Joe nodded.

"And Allie, this gentleman is Joe Hicks. He's a businessman out of Southern California. He's a new client of mine who will be living in the guesthouse for several months. You will see him frequently so you might as well play nice."

A client of hers?

Allie thought about her mother's various clients over the years. She thought of her own clients in seedy little motel rooms across Texas.

"What *kind* of client?" she asked.

"Well, as your caseworker explained when you got here, I'm a wellness practitioner. I teach unhealthy people to become healthy through diet and lifestyle. I'm going to help Joe here lose some weight and regain his good health."

Wellness practitioner? She'd never heard of that. It didn't sound like a real job. The people she'd always known had normal jobs. They waited tables, drove trucks, sold sex for cash.

The door to the attached mudroom opened and a man walked in. "Good morning, Louis," the old woman called. "Come sit. I have people for you to meet."

The man kissed Miss Bitty on the cheek, then went to the table.

"Coffee?" she asked.

"Sure."

As Louis sat, the old woman poured coffee and made the introductions. "Louis, this is Joe Hicks. He's my new out-of-state client and he'll be staying here about six months. And Joe, this is Louis. He's my right-hand man. He does a little of everything around here and also tutors a handful of students in the area, including any foster children I might be caring for."

"Nice to meet you, buddy," Louis said.

The two men shook hands.

"You, too." Joe smiled, his cheeks pink.

"And Louis, this young lady is Allie. She's the new foster child I told you about. She'll be staying with me until the right forever home is found for her."

Louis smiled at Allie. "Nice to meet you."

Allie covered the right side of her face with her hand and quickly studied the man. He was middle-aged with brown hair that was salt and pepper around the hairline. Kind, brown eyes grinned at her from behind stylish eyeglasses. He was kind of handsome in an old guy sort of way.

Allie'd had a few clients on the road who had looked a lot like him. They were the type who seemed out of place at a truck stop; the type who left as soon as it was over. Oddly enough, she'd found that the more professional the client appeared, the dirtier his fantasies had usually been.

Miss Bitty's hands went to her hips. "Allie? Louis just spoke to you."

Allie emerged from her thoughts. She shifted in her seat. "So?"

"So, you speak back. Be polite."

"Fine. Hi," she said, trying her best to sound bored. Quickly swiping sweat from her forehead with the back of her wrist, she tried to seem in control.

Anxiety attacks were the worst.

"That's better," the old woman said. "Allie, Louis here is going to be your mentor. He's going to work with you three mornings a week until you're ready to take your GED. He'll also discuss different areas of interest you might want to pursue and drive you to any appointments that conflict with my work schedule."

The refrigerator hummed in the distance as the old woman awaited a reaction. "Allie?"

"Okay."

"Louis will also be here for you if you ever want to talk about anything you're not comfortable coming to me with," the old woman continued. "Also anything you don't feel comfortable sharing with your therapist. I've known Louis long enough to know that he's an incredible listener. He won't judge, no matter how bad you think something is. How does that sound, girlie?"

Allie shrugged.

The old woman slid a glass of something green in front of Joe. He flinched. "What is this?"

"Mango, bananas, spinach, gelatin, and a couple of supplements. It's called a green smoothie. It's quite tasty, and it's going to be a staple of your diet for the next several months."

"It's actually good, man," Louis said. "Seriously. You'll be surprised."

The big man smelled it, then reluctantly took a sip. He raised his eyebrows. "Mmm, it *is* good."

The old woman glanced at Allie. "Want one?"

Allie grimaced.

"Suit yourself."

Bitty went to the island and poured some water into a glass, then set it in front of Allie with two pills.

Allie frowned. "Why so many pills all the time? Are you trying to drug me or something?"

Miss Bitty grinned. "Oh, heavens no. What would make you say that?"

"What are they then?"

"Well, let's see. I've given you the medication the doctor prescribed and some additional supplements. After what you've been through, your body is very weak. It's just screaming for nutritional support."

Nutritional what?

57

Allie felt someone's stare from across the table. She hated to be looked at, much less stared at. It made her skin crawl. She looked up and saw it was the big guy, Joe. *Big Joe.*

She pierced him with her eyes. "So, how fat are you?" she asked, knowing that if she put him on the defensive about himself, he wouldn't see all the things that were wrong with *her.*

Joe's face tightened. "I'm sorry?"

"Allie, that's no way to speak to—" Bitty started.

"I weigh 290. Why do you ask?"

Bitty's tone was firm. "I don't like how you're speaking to Joe. I want you to apologize."

But Allie didn't. "So what you're saying is that when you get done with him, he won't be so fat anymore? And people actually *pay* you for that?" She was still intent on deflecting, but the words felt bitter leaving her mouth.

Big Joe's eyes lingered on hers before dropping back to his iPad, but Allie knew he wasn't looking at anything. The screen had already gone black.

Bitty pursed her lips and threw Joe an apologetic look. "Poor thing wasn't taught any manners. Sorry about that, Joe. Obviously she doesn't know any better . . . *yet.*"

"I know better," Allie snapped. *I'm not stupid!* And it wasn't that she liked being mean. She just had to be . . . to protect herself.

Bitty looked pointedly at her. "Then why on God's earth would you purposely be so cruel?"

Allie felt her cheeks flush but said nothing. She looked away from the old woman and found herself looking straight at Louis, who was sipping coffee and watching her curiously.

"I asked you a question," Miss Bitty said.

Allie glared at the woman. She wished she had some vodka. She'd been dry now for days. If she'd been armed with a few shots, it would've been easy to think of a witty comeback. But again, she was coming up with nothing.

"I'm waiting," Miss Bitty said, her eyes steady on Allie's. The kitchen was so quiet Allie could hear Big Joe's labored breathing.

The old woman finally spoke. "Look, I'll let it go this time. Consider it a gift. But I want you to listen to me, and listen to me well. You are expected to be kind and respectful to everyone in this house. We have an understanding?"

Allie ignored the woman.

"It's okay," Joe muttered. "It's not like it's the first time. Pretty, thin people just don't get it. Especially females. And, after all these years, I honestly don't expect them to."

Bitty frowned at Joe. "Pretty? Who are you calling pretty? Allie here?"

"Well, yeah."

The woman shook her head. "No. Pretty is as pretty does. And I'd say that right now Allie is rather ugly."

Allie's throat went dry.

Why would she say that? Allie wondered. No one, except her mother, had ever openly questioned her looks before. No one else had ever called her ugly.

Her mind flashed back to how she'd looked when she'd arrived. Her makeup had been both slept in and sweated off. Yes, she'd arrived looking repulsive.

Yes, that was it.

Well, hopefully.

After all, if people began to see through her mask, what would become of her? Perceived beauty was the only thing about her of value. Well, that and her good body. But unfortunately, there *was* nothing else.

"That said, now that I have the three of you together," Miss Bitty announced, walking to the head of the table, "there's a very important rule we need to make sure we're straight on. Now that I'm caring for a female minor here, at no time do I want any males alone in the house with her after dark. If I'm here, great. You're welcome to come in. If I'm not, you will *not* be welcome inside. Do we have an understanding?"

Louis nodded. "Absolutely."

"Absolutely," Joe repeated.

The woman was staring at her again. "You got that, Allie? No boys in the house after dark. No exceptions."

Allie glared at the old woman. "Why are you going through all this trouble? Giving me that bedroom? The bathroom? Taking me shopping for clothes?" she asked, her tone icy. "Is it money? How much do you make off of me anyway?"

"Not enough for me to listen to that mouth of yours."

Allie frowned. "Then . . . why do you want me here?"

The woman paused, seemingly taken aback by the question. Then she narrowed her eyes. "Well, to help you, of course. Why else would you be here?"

CHAPTER 13

HALF AN HOUR later, Allie was in her new therapist's office. She'd expected a man, but when the door to the small waiting room swung open, a redheaded woman peeked out.

The woman smiled at her, reminding her of a piranha. "You must be Allie. I'm Renee. Come on in."

Allie remained seated, sizing the woman up. She was in her thirties . . . pretty and slim, with long red hair. She looked classy and professional. Another woman who obviously had her shit together. Renee was definitely the type who would've shunned Allie if she had met her on the street.

There was no way in hell Allie was going to talk to her.

Miss Bitty patted her shoulder. "Go on. She won't bite."

A minute later, Allie reluctantly sat on a plump couch in the woman's office, listening to the cool air as it hissed from the air-conditioning vent above them.

"Would you like some water?" Renee asked.

"No." Allie watched the woman pour herself a glass, then settle into a chair.

She picked up a file and a pen, then her eyes met Allie's. "Okay, then. Let's get started. First off, I want you to know that unless

I feel your life or someone else's is at risk, I will *not* repeat anything you share with me during these sessions. Not with your foster mother and not with your caseworker. That means that whatever you tell me during our sessions is strictly between you and me. Do you understand?"

Allie shrugged. "I guess."

In the span of just a few seconds, the woman's perfectly symmetrical face went from calm and clinical to a little sad. "Second of all, I want you to know that I can only imagine what you've gone through."

The back of Allie's neck grew hot. She highly doubted the woman could even *begin* to imagine her life. If her high-class appearance was any indication of what kind of family she'd been born into, she'd had it good. Real good. "Oh really?" she challenged, her pulse quickening. "You can?"

The woman frowned.

"You said you could imagine what I went through."

"Well, that's not exactly what I—"

"Was your mother an alcoholic?"

The calm, "I-have-my-shit-together" expression quickly returned. "No, Allie. I can't say she was."

"No? Well then, was she a whore?"

The woman didn't respond. The only sound in the room was the hiss of the air conditioner.

"Was your mother sick?"

The woman just watched her.

"Are you having a hard time understanding my questions?" Allie asked, pressing her lips flat. She formed her next words slowly, as though she were speaking to a moron. "I asked, 'Was. Your. Mother. Sick?'"

"Well, if what you mean is—"

"*What I mean* is, was she sick in the head? Did she hear things that weren't there?"

"No, Allie, she wasn't. And she didn't."

Allie wondered exactly what the woman knew about her past. About her family. She wondered if Renee had lived in the area when all the shit hit the fan. When everyone realized all the murders that had been committed right in their backyards, beneath their noses.

The murdered truck drivers.

The murdered writer.

That her brother had killed two teenaged girls, the owner of the local diner, and his own mother less than a year earlier.

Did she know any of it? Maybe *all* of it? Through clenched teeth, she asked, "Have you ever watched someone die?"

"Allie, we should—"

"Hey, I'm still talking," she interrupted, "and I want to know if you can say *yes* to any of the questions I just asked."

"I can't."

"Well, *I* can. My mother was and did *all* of those things," Allie said, her voice even louder, her harsh tone startling even herself. "And she really screwed up my brother, who meant everything in the world to me . . . so he killed himself. Right in front of me . . . he blew his head off. Then he bled all over me." Tears gathered in her eyes, and she tried to blink them away. "But I guess you can imagine what that was like, too, right?"

The woman's shoulders slumped and she didn't look so sure of herself anymore.

"My point is, you can't even *begin* to imagine what I went through," Allie said. "And if I were you I wouldn't even try, because it might hurt so much you'd wish you were dead."

Allie stood and left the room.

CHAPTER 14

ALLIE WAS RELIEVED the old woman didn't grill her about the therapy session. In fact, Miss Bitty told her that if she didn't want to go again, she didn't have to. That she'd find a way to get around the mandatory sessions. Then, she took Allie shopping.

After spending several anxiety-provoking hours in the mall, Allie stood alone in her bedroom and stared at her new clothes. On the way home, she had warned the old woman not to throw her old clothes away. "Because the minute I get myself out of here—"

"It's all in safekeeping," Miss Bitty assured her. "You're free to look as trampy as you wish when you go. For now, though, I'm not running a whorehouse and I won't let you walk around here looking like one."

Allie had blinked, wondering if her file had mentioned that she'd grown up in a whorehouse.

Or that she'd once been a whore.

At the mall, they'd bought tank tops and tees, underwear, bras, socks, jeans, shorts, dress pants, a skirt, a little black dress, and a swimsuit. Shoes that fit her: tennis shoes, sandals, flip-flops, wedges, and a pair of heels. A couple of simple necklaces, a pair of earrings, and a watch. They'd even bought her expensive department store makeup to replace the cheap stuff she'd always gotten from dollar stores.

While they were shopping, Allie had nodded off twice on the straight-back chairs the stores kept near the fitting rooms. She'd tried not to but couldn't help it. She was still lethargic, and all the stimulation of the big crowds, the hum of a hundred conversations throughout the wide aisles, pelted her brain like pressure waves.

Then there were the endless mirrors and harsh fluorescent lighting, all of which frightened her. Her heart had raced so hard for so long, she was completely drained.

Several times throughout the afternoon, people walked up to the old woman to say hello. The people always looked really happy to see Miss Bitty. They'd talk for a couple of minutes, then the old lady would resume her shopping, Allie reluctantly trailing behind her. Later, Miss Bitty explained that the people were clients—some current, some past.

When they finally returned to the house, Bitty had shown Allie how to neatly fold some of her clothing and how to properly hang the rest. But as soon as the old woman left the room, Allie locked the door and pulled everything out again.

She couldn't get over seeing it all right there, in one place, on the bed. Everything fit well and was brand-spanking new . . . and all of it was *hers*.

She posed in front of the bathroom mirror, modeling her new clothes, careful to only look at the good side of her face. For once, she actually looked well put together. Almost like the pretty therapist, Renee.

I look nice. Like, for once, I actually look like I have class.

The new image of herself made her almost breathless.

But then she remembered who she really was.

She shrugged off the clothes, put everything back as neatly as it had been before, and crawled into bed. But she made sure to leave the folding closet doors wide open just so she could see the clothes as she fell asleep.

She loved them all, every single piece, but knew that they would never truly be hers, because she'd been taught better than to trust the old woman. She was too kind. Too generous. She hadn't even yelled at her once . . . and she really, genuinely paid attention to her. All of that and she didn't even ask for anything in return.

She seems too good to be true . . . which could only mean one thing: she was.

———

A summer storm was raging outside when something summoned Allie from a sound sleep. Exhausted, she was tempted to ignore whatever it was and slip down deeper beneath the covers.

But she sensed someone's presence.

Opening her eyes, she sat up and saw Miss Bitty standing in the doorway.

"What's going on?" Allie asked, irritated to have been woken.

Miss Bitty didn't answer.

Allie frowned in the darkness. "Is everything okay?"

Nothing. Just the sound of raindrops striking the bedroom window.

Her pulse quickened and she sat up straight. "Miss Bitty? Is that you?" She squinted to try to get a better look, but it was too dark in the room. Frightened, she clung to the comforter.

Lightening flashed outside, briefly illuminating the room. But the doorway was empty. Allie exhaled, wondering if she'd only imagined someone had been there.

Thunder crashed in the distance and her grip on the comforter softened. She watched the doorway for several more minutes, until she was certain no one was there.

I'm just losing it. No one was ever there, she told herself. *My God, what is wrong with me?*

She lay back down and squeezed her eyes shut, willing her pulse to return to normal. She was just exhausted . . . and her imagination was running wild.

Pulling the covers more tightly around her, she listened to the rain strike her window and soon fell into a restless sleep.

CHAPTER 15

UNABLE TO SLEEP, Miss Bitty stepped into the rain-cleansed air. She walked barefoot to the garden to knead her weathered feet in the cool mud. The practice was called earthing, and it was something she often did when her sense of tranquility eluded her.

After she quit drinking, years ago, she'd turned to practices like earthing for the type of calmness a bottle of wine had provided those many years when she'd been a closet drunk.

Usually it did the trick.

Usually.

As the late-night breeze ruffled her hair, she studied her garden in the moonlight and let the cool mud sink between her toes. She'd been toying with strategies to get Allie to trust her. From what she'd gathered thus far, the girl was very intelligent, so it wouldn't take much to raise suspicion. She'd have to be calculating.

But that wasn't all that was concerning her. A sick feeling had bloomed in her gut earlier in the day. Something horrific was on the horizon. Something that could ruin everything.

The entire well-laid plan.

She had a gift few were aware of: she *knew* things. Sometimes she knew before events happened. Sometimes *as* they were happening.

And the knowledge always began with the same twisted feeling in the pit of her gut.

The problem was that she never got the complete picture—and sometimes this made her desperate, especially when she intuited something that was so dangerously close to home . . . like she was now.

She walked around the house until she found herself outside the girl's bedroom window and wondered if she was asleep. Peering at her watch, she realized it was nearly half past three in the morning, so she figured Allie was.

A warm breeze tickled her neck, making the hair on her arms and legs stand on end. She pulled the robe tighter against her body and walked back to the house.

CHAPTER 16

TEN MINUTES LATER, Allie jackknifed to a sitting position. She gathered her breath, trying to get her bearings.

Something had awoken her again. She stole a look at the doorway. To her relief, it was still empty. She glanced at the bedside clock: 3:40 a.m. The brunt of the storm seemed to have passed and now the branches outside her window were swaying in the wind, casting long, eerie shadows on the bedroom's walls.

With the moon shining through the bedroom window, she could make out the soft outlines of some of the clothes hanging in the closet. She groaned and peeled back the covers.

Something wasn't right. She couldn't put her finger on it . . . but she didn't think she should stay long enough to find out. She was too smart to believe that Miss Bitty was only trying to help her. No one in their right mind would go out of their way so much to help her. Besides, she didn't belong here.

Although she had no idea *where* (if anywhere) she belonged, she knew it wasn't in the old woman's squeaky-clean house, living some charade until everyone figured out who and what she really was. Even if the woman did have good intentions, it would only be a matter of time before she realized she didn't want her around, and Allie didn't think she could handle more abandonment.

Allie went to the window and pressed a palm against the warm glass. She was pretty sure she knew her way home. She used to know the woods like the back of her hand, having gone on adventures with her brother as a kid.

She went to the closet, pulled on the new tennis shoes, and packed a few of her new things into the backpack since the old woman had stored away most of what she'd come with. Then, back at the window, she carefully pushed the screen out of the pane.

Hopping out, she darted across the backyard and disappeared into the murky woods.

———

Allie sat on the cement steps that led from the back door of her childhood house.

Although the late-night air was warm, she shivered as she stared in the direction of the pond at the edge of the property. As a little girl, she had spent many years swimming in it and running along its grassy bank. That was, of course, before she realized that several human bodies were decomposing beneath its smooth surface.

Unfortunately, she'd learned about them the hard way.

It had been a scorching afternoon. She was out shooting water moccasins with her brother's pellet gun and had just pulled off her tennis shoes and begun wading in the cool water when she noticed the first one: the pale, bloated body of what appeared to be a man. He was floating on the surface less than a yard from her. But just as she began to scream, a hand gripped her shoulder.

Her mother's hand.

"You will keep your mouth shut if you want me to love you," the woman warned, her teeth clenched tightly. She pinched Allie's shoulder hard, then let go and waded into the murky water, toward the body. She called over her shoulder, "And don't you dare even think about judging me. Because you'll turn out no different than me, Allie Cat. Wait. You'll see." Then, as though it had been an afterthought: "Of course, things will be even harder for you . . . with that strange little face of yours." She grimaced. "How I made such an ugly child is beyond me."

Allie tried to shake off the memory of her mother's words. Words she thought about much too often.

She hadn't been inside the house yet. She wasn't ready. It had taken her thirty minutes on foot to reach the house and having traveled through wet, tree-filled ravines, she had ruined her new shoes.

An early-morning breeze kicked up, rattling a loose windowpane in the kitchen. She was still staring at her mud-splattered shoestrings when a sound came from the pond. She froze and listened closely. She heard it again: a woman screaming. Gooseflesh rising on her arms, Allie jumped up. Pulling open the screen door, she hurried through the kitchen and down the hallway.

Back in her brother's musty room, she crawled into the bed and curled into a tight ball. Trembling, she wondered, not for the first time, if her mother had been right. She *was* becoming just like her, wasn't she? She was starting to see things . . . hear things. Things she honestly doubted were actually there.

I'm losing it.

And I'm all alone.

An intense loneliness washed over her and she suddenly wished she were back at the old woman's house. Tears filled her eyes as she finally accepted the fact she was out of options.

She wouldn't be able to live in the house without electricity and water. She had no skills to offer an employer . . . and she could never go back to selling herself.

Something clattered in front of the house. Allie stiffened and strained to listen but couldn't hear anything.

A few minutes later, the wind started screaming on the other side of the window. Allie's thoughts shifted to the many nights she'd lain in the very same bed, cocooned beneath the blankets with her brother, trying not to hear the violent weather *inside* the house.

She hated when she'd gotten too old to lay in bed with him. When she was thirteen, he began turning her away. "You're too old for this," he said. "It's just not right. Go sleep in your own bed. Go, now. Before Mother finds out you've been in here."

But the rejection had been unbearable—and only led her to new appeals. Eventually she had the brilliant idea of trying to emulate the pictures in the dirty magazines: pictures he'd been so obsessed with; pictures he'd spent hours looking at and then ripping up. Only now did she realize her mistake. The girls in his magazines that she copied were girls he loathed. His fixation for them had nothing to do with adoration or love. It had to do with hate . . . which was probably a big part of why he'd begun to hate her, too. She made him uncomfortable. Miserable even.

What she had done had been so incredibly wrong.

So incredibly stupid.

For the next two hours she lay curled up in the filthy bed. She would lie there until the morning, until she was able to figure out what to do next.

The steady purr of a motor stirred Allie from her sleep. Her eyes popped open beneath the covers, and she remembered where she was and knew what was about to happen.

The Department of Children and Family Services was there to take her in again, and this time they'd find her a new foster home.

Probably one that was truly terrible like her caseworker had warned. Her first instinct was to run, but she didn't because there was absolutely no place to go.

The screen door to the front of the small house squeaked open. Then there were footsteps and a familiar voice.

"Allie? You in here?"

It was Miss Bitty.

Allie's pulse quickened. She sat up and wiped her eyes.

"Allie? It's me, girlie. Are you here?"

Don't trust her, something warned inside her head. But Allie ignored it. She climbed out of the bed and moved into the dark hallway. Bitty shined a flashlight on the wall to help light her path. "Come on, sweetheart. Let's get you home."

Home?

She didn't even think before talking next. "What if I don't want to go back there?"

"I happen to think you do," the woman said, her voice gentle. "Don't try so hard to be tough. Please. Accept my help."

Allie paused. "If I go back with you, are you going to call them to come and get me?" she asked.

"What? Call whom?"

"My caseworker. DCFS."

"Why would I do that?"

"Because you're angry at me."

"Why would you think that? I'm not angry."

Allie stared at the woman. "But I've been trouble for you. Why *wouldn't* you be angry?"

"It was a short drive, girlie," Bitty said. "Besides, I get it. It's just going to take some time. Now c'mon. Let's get you home, cleaned up, and into your bed."

What? How could she possibly not be angry?

"I still don't know why you're going out of your way to help me," Allie said, her voice coming out much more squeaky than she'd hoped. "What are you getting out of it?"

"I think everyone deserves some help when they're down. Don't you? And if it makes you more comfortable, I have no problem making you work for it." The woman put the flashlight up to her old face so Allie could see her wink.

What do I have to lose? Allie asked herself. *Nothing.*

But Allie shook her head. "No, I want you to be honest with me," she said, sounding more confident than she felt. "None of the bullshit. Why are you helping me?"

The woman was silent for a long moment. Finally, she sighed. "Can you keep a secret?"

"Yes."

"Okay, well, if you must know, I've done something bad. Something really, truly awful and I'm trying to make up for it the only way I know how."

Allie processed the old woman's words. She sounded so honest and heartfelt it was hard not to believe her. Maybe the woman *had* done something truly bad. If she had, that was okay. There was no way she'd done anything worse than Allie had. She'd practically killed her brother. If it wasn't for her being so hateful to him, he'd possibly still be alive.

Bitty suddenly seemed more real to her. Maybe she really was going to help her. Maybe she could *really* give her a new life. Maybe it would be okay to believe her . . . at least for now.

"Now c'mon, you," the old woman said. "Let's stop talking and get you home." She reached out to take Allie's hand.

And, for the first time, Allie let her.

CHAPTER 17

HE'D GOTTEN ATTACHED. He'd only visited Hope a handful of times—but already he thought about her all the time.

No matter where he was.

No matter whom he was with.

With Hope, he suddenly felt like he wouldn't have to kill to relieve himself of the itch. With Hope he felt that stalking might finally be enough to get him by.

He should've known Hope was going somewhere when she didn't post a new waitressing schedule on the refrigerator. He should've stopped her.

But she was out of town now and he was a mess. Since she'd been gone, he hadn't been able to sleep or eat. He couldn't even think straight. The itch had returned, just beneath his skin. Just beneath his scalp and between the fragile skin of his fingers and toes.

Everything seemed darker.

More hopeless.

Little things were beginning to set him off. Practically everything SHE said to him grated on his nerves. He was pretty sure he was even starting to hate HER. But it wouldn't be the first time. He had hated HER before.

Squeezing his eyes shut, he tried to calm down. He replayed a well-worn memory. The memory of his first hunt . . .

The eleventh grade. A chilly October evening close to dinner-time. The sun was low in the sky. He was walking home along a fairly populated bike path when a girl whizzed by on a pink ten-speed, then took a tumble on a tree branch that was stretched across the asphalt. He remembered it like it was yesterday . . . how she flew over the handlebars, landed with a thud, and skidded to a stop. When he walked over to her, he realized who she was. Kimberly Ribby. Pretty . . . popular. As he studied her features up close, his hands became fists. A year earlier she had helped a friend humiliate him.

He offered to walk her home. He walked with her bike as she hobbled beside him for several feet before they cut through the woods to get to her house.

He remembered how he'd began to sweat once they entered the woods. How alone they suddenly were. Without much conscious thought at all, he threw the bike down and grabbed her by the throat. Then he dragged her deeper into the woods and strangled her with his bare hands.

For seven years after that evening he felt a little more certain of himself. A little less impotent. He even became a fairly productive adult, one who most people seemed to like well enough. For once it wasn't so difficult to fit in.

During those seven years, the anger still came and went, but it was finally manageable. And for the most part, he felt normal. He thought for sure he'd been healed. That the rest of his life would be a piece of cake. But around the seven-year mark, the itch started. The itch to do it again . . .

Snapping back to the present, he realized that the memory no longer soothed him like it once had. In fact it only made him angrier.

He had to do *something*.

Suddenly a light went on in his head. He'd pay the teenage girl a visit.

He weighed the idea, knowing it would be risky. Last time he'd almost gotten caught. The girl had awoken and, in the darkness, had called out to him, thinking he was the old lady. It had been a very close call. But he was willing to do it again.

For the first time in his life he was getting sloppy. It was almost as though a part of him, one he didn't have access to, *wanted* to get caught.

And that seriously disturbed him.

———

It was two o'clock in the morning when he eased the young girl's door open.

He was sweating profusely and he itched all over.

He was desperate for relief.

He had tried to stay away from the teenager but had failed. She was much different than Hope. Different than the brunette. Terribly different than *any* of them. She didn't just *remind* him of the type of girl who'd scorned him when he was a boy, *she was the spitting image of her*. The spitting image of the type who had humiliated him. While other boys were busy fantasizing about luring this type of girl into bed, he only fantasized about hurting her.

But there was something more about *this* girl. Something that made it equally as tempting to be close to her. To discover exactly how she affected him.

Sweat beading on his upper lip, he let his eyes adjust before stepping closer to the bed. Then, staring down at her, he studied her features.

Her long, dark hair was splayed neatly across her pillow. Her face was relaxed. She looked even younger while she was sleeping, and so vulnerable with her mouth slightly parted, covers drawn up to her chin. *Absolutely gorgeous.*

As he watched, a slender, sun-browned leg slipped out from beneath the covers to rest on the fitted sheet.

He was surprised that being so close to her didn't make him angry.

At least, not yet.

Straightening his spine, he vowed not to hurt her—not intentionally anyway, although sometimes he certainly didn't seem to be the one in control.

No. This one, he had special plans for. His pulse raced just thinking about them. He watched the girl for a little while longer, until she grunted and rolled over.

By the time she settled again, he was gone, more frustrated than when he'd arrived.

CHAPTER 18

DESPERATE, HE RETURNED to Sherwood Foods. He scanned women for hours, but no one came close to interesting him.

Until the beautiful brunette with the Pathfinder returned.

The one with the young son.

He was standing in his usual place, nauseous and itching all over, when she hurried her son into the store. But when she rushed past, completely ignoring him, he realized he needed to take matters into his own hands.

He entered the supermarket and watched her and the boy at a distance as they shopped. She only threw a few items in her basket before dashing to a checkout line, so he knew his window of opportunity was going to be small. He wasn't certain what to do. He just knew he couldn't wait any longer. He needed to make something happen.

So he left the supermarket and walked to her vehicle. Once he reached it, he whirled around and headed slowly back toward the supermarket doors.

Perfect timing. The woman and kid were just exiting the automatic doors. He walked toward them, trying to keep his breathing in check. To look normal.

When they were just a few feet away, his eyes met hers. He grinned and stopped. "Cheryl? Cheryl Robicheaux?"

He purposely stood in the woman's path. Annoyed, she stopped and frowned. "No. Wrong person."

Through his nausea, he smiled as widely as he could. "No? C'mon! But you're the spitting image of her."

The woman stared at him.

"C'mon, Mom," the boy said.

"Excuse me. We're in a hurry," the woman said. She grabbed her son's hand.

So much for smiles being infectious. His own slipped off his face. "Oh, well, sorry to have bothered you," he said, stepping out of the woman's way.

She and the boy continued to the vehicle.

Wiping his damp brow, he tried to think quickly. He needed somehow to make the woman smile.

Desperate, he spun around. "Miss?"

The woman turned, her eyes flashing. "Yes?"

"It's a beautiful day. Surely you have something to smile about, right?" he asked, trying to sound light amid the rage bubbling in his belly. "Something, right? *Anything?*"

The woman scowled at him. Right before she turned to get into her vehicle, though, she threw him a strained smile. A sarcastic one.

Charity.

But it was enough. He was desperate.

Hurrying to his vehicle, he caught up with her as she left the shopping center and sped south. He was still following her, not five minutes later, as she pulled the Pathfinder into her driveway.

CHAPTER 19

AFTER THE SUN set, he sat, nauseous, in his vehicle and watched the brunette woman's little ranch house, waiting for the last two lights to go out.

He recalled how rude and impatient she had been with him and his breath hitched. He thought of the little schoolgirls when he was a boy—and how merciless they'd been with him, too. He hadn't fit in and they had taken it upon themselves to make sure he didn't forget it . . . not even for a second.

The memories flooded his head so quickly it felt like it was going to explode. Hateful kids who made him feel inferior, ugly, awkward, uncomfortable, inconsequential, and alienated. Year after year, over and over, it had been the same thing. He'd hated them all, but *mostly* the girls.

They were the ones who hurt him most.

The disgust he'd learned to feel for himself was overwhelming. He was different and he didn't want to be. He felt inferior and that infuriated him.

Realizing he had the steering wheel in a death grip, he forced himself to think of something less anxiety provoking . . . and found himself wondering about the brunette's son. About what type of life he lived. If the boy had ever experienced anything like he had in school. Also, if there was a father in the picture.

The kid had appeared pretty normal in the supermarket. But he knew from experience that even the sickest of people could *appear* normal.

After contemplating the boy for a little while, he sank back into his seat and thought about his own family.

He'd come from a fine family by today's standards. He'd never been molested or been a victim of incest. He'd never been chronically ridiculed by an authority figure. He had lived in the same house until he was nine and always felt a certain degree of stability, he supposed.

And life had gotten even better once his father left and he was alone with his mom. When his father had lived with them, the man had always been a distraction, so he barely got to even talk to his mom. Instead, she had been so focused on keeping her husband at home, happy, and somewhat involved with the family that her son's needs often fell to the wayside, even though her husband had rarely been emotionally available to either of them.

He couldn't remember suffering any significant childhood trauma at home, outside of a few spankings from his father. But those had been few and far between—and were of no consequence to him, long term. He never much cared for his father anyway. In fact, as hard as he'd tried when he was younger, he'd never seen even one redeeming quality in the man.

He closed his eyes. What *had* been of consequence, he knew, had been the emotional (and sometimes physical) beatings from his classmates at school. Words that inevitably shaped his own opinion of himself. Opinions that he'd tried unsuccessfully to shed through-out his life. But still, his experiences were nothing unique. Kids got picked on all over the world. Some kids had low esteem and natu-rally believed the worst about themselves. So on most accounts, his childhood was pretty normal.

But he'd come to realize at a very young age that there was something different about him . . . something terribly wrong. Maybe the other kids had sensed it before he did, and that's why they'd treated him so badly.

He continued to watch the woman's house. At exactly 11:30 p.m., the last of the lights went out and the house was bathed in darkness.

Throwing his vehicle into gear, he drove to a secluded area three blocks away to park. Then he got out of the car and walked toward the house.

CHAPTER 20

THE INSIDE OF the brunette's house smelled of household cleaner and cheap perfume.

Aside from the dull glow of a lamp on an end table and a wall-mounted night-light in the hallway, all the lights had been switched off.

He trained his flashlight around the room. Fresh vacuum tracks were etched into the living-room carpet, and the air held the subtle burnt odor of an old vacuum cleaner. The woman had cleaned before going to bed.

Little blonde Hope could learn some things from her.

Keeping his flashlight low, he slinked through the living room and into the hallway, grasping his hunting knife.

A bedroom door to his right was ajar. He peered in and saw the outline of someone lying in a bed. His grip tightened on the knife and he slowly entered. It was the preteen boy's room. The kid lay on his back, his comforter a puddle at the end of his bed, his mouth wide open in sleep. He watched the boy's chest and its rhythmic rise and fall. Music whispered from a laptop on a desk. He recognized the upbeat song: "Teenage Dream" by Katy Perry.

Fitting.

The boy stirred, then licked his lips and turned onto his side. The man watched until he was certain the boy was sound asleep again; then he left the room and gently closed the door.

The next room was an office, with a desk covered with files and a flat-screen computer monitor. In the corner was a tall, metal filing cabinet. There was also a chest of drawers and a rocking chair. Photos on the walls revealed happy times between the mother and child. He trained his flashlight on everything, trying to get a sense of who this woman was.

As he moved his light to the other side of the room, his heart nearly leapt out of his chest. A dog sat silently on the floor, just inches away, staring up at him.

Jesus!

He tightened his grip on the knife and readied himself. But the dog just stared at him and, strangely, continued to do nothing.

He blinked in the darkness—and suddenly realized the dog was behaving oddly . . . sitting *too* still.

He took a step forward and, again, the dog did nothing.

It wasn't real.

It was stuffed.

He wiped more sweat from his brow and took a couple of minutes to calm down. Then he returned to the hallway and checked out the next room.

This room was twice as big. It was the master bedroom. The woman's room. His synapses fired with extra intensity as he crossed the doorway.

Hunting was what he truly lived for . . . it was what kept him from exploding daily in uncontrolled environments. It's what helped him maintain a mask of normalcy in his daily life. Hunting was truly the only thing he ever looked forward to. He hungered for it like others hungered for food.

Hunting made him who he wished he was . . . for a while.

Who he pretended to be.

It was the only thing that made him feel truly alive.

He moved deeper into the room and found the woman sleeping on top of her covers. He stepped closer and inhaled her scent. Catching a hint of a flowery lotion, he bent closer and tried to decipher the odor beneath it. To know what her skin smelled like beneath all of the fake flowers. But the lotion was too strong.

Tilting his head, he watched her for a long while as she breathed. Excitement building, he considered clamping his hand against her mouth. To immobilize her and—

No . . . not now.

After all, he was already feeling more relaxed. He felt exhilarated, but calm. Just knowing that killing her was within his power had brought him a little relief, albeit temporary—just as it had with Hope.

The thought popped into his mind again. Maybe, just maybe, he really *had* evolved over the years and he could get by with just stalking them this time. Medicating himself solely with the thrill of anticipation. Hunting them, then letting them go. Like fisherman did with fish: catch and release.

Maybe, just maybe, he could feed his addiction without risking losing HER.

Could it really be possible?

Maybe, he thought, deciding to be cautiously optimistic.

Blinking rapidly, he watched the woman sleep for several minutes and vowed to try. He bent down close to her again until he was just a few inches from her skin and committed her scent to memory.

Then he forced himself to leave the room.

CHAPTER 21

THE SUN HAD only been up a couple of hours when Allie wandered into the kitchen to the scent of coffee brewing and Miss Bitty, Big Joe, and Louis talking at the table. When they noticed her, they fell silent.

That morning she'd chosen one of her new shorts outfits and had spent some time French braiding her hair. She'd also applied the makeup Miss Bitty had bought her and was careful to tone it down because the old woman had told her that the way she wore it made her look cheap. Instead of her usual cherry-red lipstick, she'd chosen an understated lip gloss. Instead of slathering on the black eyeliner like she usually did, she only used a little brown.

The old woman said she saw good in her. And that gave Allie hope. She still didn't trust Miss Bitty completely, but she was trying to. After all, the woman could be planning to use her as an indentured servant and it still wouldn't be nearly as bad as the life Allie had lived. As a thank-you to the old woman for forgiving her and letting her stay, Allie had dressed more conservatively. And she must've succeeded because she saw a glint of approval in Miss Bitty's eyes.

"You get a makeover?" Big Joe asked. "You look . . . fantastic."

Well, not exactly fantastic, but better, maybe, she thought.

"Yes, you look very lovely," Miss Bitty agreed.

Miss Bitty finally stood and grabbed a pitcher. "Well, don't just stand there. Come, sit."

Her face burning beneath everyone's still-appraising eyes, Allie sat where Miss Bitty had been sitting and concentrated on the juice pouring into her glass.

"Freshly squeezed spinach, celery, apple. Soon to be one of *your* morning chores." Bitty winked.

Chores. She'd never had chores before. The previous evening, Miss Bitty had explained what was going to be expected of her. On top of being responsible for a number of daily chores, Allie was going to help Bitty with client paperwork. The old woman had even found her a job: cashiering at a supermarket, two shifts a week.

Allie had never had a job before either—at least, not a legitimate one that came with a paycheck. The idea made her both anxious and excited.

She was also going to be homeschooled. "You'll start your tutoring with Louis this morning, girlie," Miss Bitty said, setting a binder, three notebooks, and a box of pens in front of her.

Allie nodded, her eyes on the school supplies. Everything was colorful, brand-new.

"You like math, Allie?" Louis asked.

"Uh, I'm not sure."

He grinned. "Well, I hope so because that's where we're going to start today."

"Okay." She tried to smile—something she hadn't done for a long time. The effort made her face feel like it was splitting in two.

———

An hour later, Allie pushed a completed assessment test across the kitchen table.

She watched Louis, who was pacing in front of the window, alternately gazing into the yard and typing on his iPhone—and thought of how quickly things had changed.

Just hours ago, she'd been certain life was pointless, and just days ago she had tried to kill herself. Now, it seemed that things were looking up in a way she never could have imagined. It was as though she were living someone else's life. It certainly didn't seem like something that could happen to her.

But it *was* happening.

Well, wasn't it?

Her mother had always told her to be suspicious of generosity, that nothing was truly ever free. But maybe she'd been wrong.

Louis looked up. "That was fast."

Allie shrugged.

Her assessment tests that morning had been surprisingly easy despite the fact that she hadn't attended school in years. Even though she had hated school, she had always loved to learn. In fact, since becoming old enough to read, she had read everything she could get her hands on.

Louis picked up her test and made some marks. A minute later, he looked up. "At this rate, it looks—"

A clatter erupted from the back of the kitchen. Allie shot to her feet, squeezed her eyes shut, and clamped her hands to her ears. Her head screamed with the memory of the gunshot, the odor of gunpowder, her brother falling to the floor.

After a few seconds, she opened her eyes to find that the noise had just been Big Joe hurrying through the mudroom door. *"Shit!"* she screamed. "Can you *not* do that?"

The big guy stopped in his tracks. "Do what?"

"Slam the door open like that!"

He frowned. "Well, I didn't mean—" he started. Then his eyes seemed to grow hard. "Sorry." He disappeared into the living room, his jug of green smoothie in hand.

"You okay?" Louis asked.

Allie nodded.

"Do loud noises frighten you?"

She shrugged, sweat cooling in the center of her back. "Yeah, I guess."

"Well, I'm sorry it scared you. He didn't mean anything by it, though. From what I know about him, the poor guy wouldn't hurt a fly."

Maybe not, but it still didn't help the fact that he had just scared the crap out of her.

"Do you read much, Allie?"

"I used to," she muttered, starting to calm down. "All the time with my broth—" She clamped her mouth shut.

Louis studied her, forcing her to look away. Lacing his fingers above his head, he sank back in his chair. "Were you going to say your 'brother'?"

Allie jerked her head forward, letting her hair fall across the side of her face. It was her ugly side—and she'd just realized it was exposed. She nodded at Louis's question, her eyes glued to the table.

"It's okay if you don't want to talk about him. But if you ever do . . . and not just about him, but about *anything* . . . I want you to know you have a safe environment here. With Miss Bitty. With me. We're both great listeners . . . and neither of us would ever judge you."

The last time she'd talked about her past was with Johnny, and just a few days afterward, he left.

"Miss Bitty is like a celebrity around here, isn't she?" Allie blurted. "So many people recognized her when we were at the mall."

Louis grinned. "Yeah. Yeah, I guess she is. When you teach someone how to regain their health, people tend to hold you in high regard. And she's helped *a lot* of people in the last year or so since she's been here."

He glanced at his watch. "Okay, let's wrap things up. I need to leave for another appointment."

He slid Allie's assessment tests across the table so she could see them. "You did really well. You are seriously one smart cookie to do so well from such little schooling. I'm sure your interest in reading helped, too."

Smart cookie?

Me?

He removed his glasses and ran a small cloth over the lenses. "From the way you tested today, it looks like we won't have nearly as much work as we thought to get you prepared for that GED."

Something in Allie's belly fluttered. No one had ever called her smart before. It definitely had a different ring to it. An awesome one.

Smart cookie . . .

"Allie? You with me?"

"Huh? Oh, yeah."

CHAPTER 22

THIRTY MINUTES AFTER Louis left, Allie was in the kitchen with her caseworker, Miss Bitty, the town's sheriff, and a female FBI agent who had identified herself as Special Agent Denise Jones.

"Like I mentioned," Agent Jones said, "my partner and I worked with Sheriff Hebert on your brother's case last year."

Allie stared past the woman's kind eyes, at the window. A man was dragging the lawn mower out of the shed. It was one of the men she'd seen the day she arrived.

"Given the circumstances, I'm sure you are going through a very difficult time. And I'm really sorry. I couldn't even imagine."

Allie kept staring out the window. Since the sheriff and the agent had shown up, she was finding it difficult to breathe.

"And I know, Allie, that you've already spoken with the sheriff here, but I want to ask a few questions, too. Is that okay?"

Allie didn't answer. She watched the man push the lawn mower in front of the window and stare in. She wondered if he could actually see them or if he was just looking at his own reflection.

After a moment, the agent continued. "Did you know Tiffany Perron and Sarah Greene? The girls who your brother killed?"

Allie's leg began to shake under the table. She didn't want to answer any questions about her brother. She didn't want to be in the same room with the sheriff, breathing the same air he breathed.

"Allie?" her caseworker prompted.

"What?" she asked, trying not to sound nervous.

"Did you know Tiffany and Sarah?" the agent asked again.

"No. I didn't know them."

"Did you know if they were friends with your brother? Or if he knew them?"

She shook her head.

"Any idea why he would want to kill them?"

Allie felt nauseous. "No. Why do you keep asking me the same questions? These are the exact same questions *he* asked me the other night," she said, gesturing to Sheriff Hebert. "I already answered them all."

Allie glared at the sheriff. She hated him. She had since she was a little girl. She remembered his afternoon visits to her mother. And from the way he studiously avoided her eyes, she was pretty sure he remembered her, too.

"We just need a better understanding of what happened," Agent Jones said gently.

"Well, I didn't know anything. I had no idea."

"No idea about . . . ?"

"Anything."

She didn't want to return to those horrible days again. Plus, she didn't owe the sheriff a damn thing. He and his department disgusted her. There had been many times when he could've helped free her and her brother from that god-awful house they'd called home. But instead he turned a blind eye because he wanted to continue visiting her mother. He didn't deserve Allie's help. She wasn't going to tell any of them shit.

"You do realize that we found several bodies on your family's property."

The hair rose on Allie's arms. "So I hear."

"I'm sorry?"

"At the hospital. The sheriff told me you found bodies."

"And you had no knowledge of them beforehand?"

"No."

"We were able to link a few of them to your mother. Did you have any knowledge that she was involved with any murders?"

"No."

The agent's voice softened. "Were you told that we found your mother's body, too? In the pond?"

Bile crawled up her throat. "Yes."

"What happened to her?"

"I don't know."

"As far as I understand, she was never reported missing."

Please . . . just leave me alone! she screamed inside her head. Talking to them about her mother . . . her brother . . . everything that had happened just made it more real. She couldn't handle it being any more real.

Allie turned to Miss Bitty. "Can we stop? Please?"

Miss Bitty jumped to her feet. "Is this really necessary? As far as I know her brother's case is closed, so I don't understand the point of you questioning her again."

The caseworker intervened. "It's better if she answers their questions now. Let's just answer them and get it over with."

"Your caseworker is right," Agent Jones said. "Now that you're back and have had a couple of days to get settled, we just want to wrap—"

"Well, let me save you a lot of time," Allie said, raising her chin in defiance. "I know nothing. *Nothing!* I had no idea my brother was involved with anything. I was as surprised as everyone else seems to be. I didn't know the girls. I didn't know *he* knew the girls. I never saw them around. How many times do I have to tell you people the same things? My story isn't going to change, because it's the truth!"

"Your mother?" the FBI agent gently prompted. "For instance, did she—"

"My mother barely had anything to do with us," Allie snapped. "One day she was there, then one day she wasn't, so I just figured she ran off with one of her clients." Allie stopped to take a breath. "Look, I barely even knew the woman. If you have questions about her, maybe you should ask Sheriff Hebert," she said, gesturing to the big man again. "Because I'm pretty sure he knew her a whole lot better than I did."

The sheriff visibly stiffened.

Agent Jones glanced at him, and he shrugged as if he didn't know what Allie was talking about, but his face was beet red. He cleared his throat. "Okay, I think that's enough for now. Thank you for talking with us. If we have anything else, we'll be back by."

Kneeling on bare knees, Allie yanked weeds out of the damp earth. Caring for Miss Bitty's organic garden was one of her many chores around the house.

The new jobs filled her with a sense of pride. She'd never really been responsible for anything before. They kept her mind busy, too, and off the sheriff's visit earlier in the day.

After working for a little more than an hour, she stood and stretched. Her head spun just thinking about the good stuff that was happening. She had decided she was going to work hard and make the old woman proud, because she knew that if she was given a second chance, she wasn't likely to be given a third.

She listened to Miss Bitty and did everything she asked. She was even drinking the green smoothies—and, as long as she threw a little apple in the blender, they were delicious.

She would also start cashiering at a supermarket soon. She fantasized about what it would be like to get paychecks.

Real ones, on paper.

Not just wadded-up bills on a nightstand.

Someone placed a hand gently on the middle of her back. "Allie?"

She jumped and peered over her shoulder, expecting to see Miss Bitty. But no one was there.

She spun around. Again, no one.

A shiver slid up her spine.

Did I just imagine that? She folded her arms across her body and held herself tightly.

"Yes," she said aloud, needing to convince herself. She *had* just imagined it. It was the only possibility because there was no way . . . no way in hell she was getting sick.

Her eyes welled up with tears. No, things were finally beginning to look up. She finally had a real chance. A chance for something normal. A chance to finally be happy.

Wiping tears from her cheek, she threw herself back into her work. "Stop screwing with me," she growled, digging harder, not sure who she was talking to . . . wondering if it could be her mother. After all, if the woman had the power to make her miserable from hell, she would do it.

Actually, it would be better if it *was* her mother because that would only mean she was being haunted. And she would much rather be haunted than crazy.

"Just let me be happy for once," she hissed. "Make someone there in hell with you miserable and leave me the fuck alone."

"I'm sorry?"

Allie froze. But she refused to turn around, hoping that if she didn't entertain whomever or whatever it was, it would eventually go away.

"Can you hear me?" the voice said.

Allie started jabbing at the broken earth again.

"Um, hello?"

She dug harder, a stream of tears warming her cheeks.

A long shadow appeared next to her. *What the—?* She whirled around, brandishing the hand shovel. "I said, get the hell—"

A girl about her age stepped backward, her eyes wide as saucers. "Oh my God. Sorry. I—"

Allie narrowed her eyes. "How long have you been standing there?"

"Uh, a few seconds, maybe?" The girl seemed confused. "Why?"

Allie quickly wiped the tears away. "What are you doing here?"

The girl gave Allie a quick, but unmistakable, once-over, then smiled confidently, showing a mouth full of perfect teeth. "My mom's inside. She came here to lose weight."

Allie weighed the girl's words. "So you're not a new foster kid?"

"Uh, not that I know of." The girl shot her another confident grin. "If only I were so lucky. My mother's a complete head case."

"Oh," Allie muttered, relieved. For a moment she had been afraid that the girl was going to take her place.

"I was just waiting for my mom and saw you. Thought I'd say hello is all."

Still suspicious, Allie studied the girl. She had long brown hair that fell past her shoulders in loose waves and gorgeous, wide-set chocolate-colored eyes. Her skin was luminous; perfect. She was exactly the type of girl you'd see on the cover of a fashion magazine.

Embarrassed by her behavior, Allie crossed her arms. She glanced past the girl and saw Miss Bitty and a woman talking on the deck.

"My name's Hannah Hanover," the girl said, pushing a mound of dirt around with her foot. "We just moved here from California and I don't really know anyone."

Allie wasn't sure what to say.

"So, you going to be a senior in August?" Hannah asked.

Allie shrugged, her eyes on the ground. "I'm not sure. I'm being homeschooled."

The girl's jaw dropped. "Get out! How cool."

Allie shrugged again.

"Wow, you're lucky. I'd love to not have to go to real school."

"Hannah!" the woman on the deck called.

The girl grunted and waved the woman off. Then she turned back to Allie. "Hey, maybe we could hang out sometime?"

Allie's heart skipped a beat. No one had ever just come up to her, wanting to hang out. To be *friends*. Allie was the weird girl. Was that not obvious to this kid? Guys were the only people interested in her—and it was only to get into her pants.

Hannah's eyes widened. "Oh, I'm not like a stalker or anything. I just don't know anyone else. But if you—"

"Sure," Allie interrupted. "We could hang out." She quickly added, "You know . . . because I don't know anyone either."

Hannah smiled. "Sweet. Okay, cool!"

"Cool," Allie repeated, feeling awkward, but also a little proud of herself for possibly making a new friend.

"So, want to come over tonight?" Hannah asked, her eyes hopeful.

Allie swallowed. "Um, yeah. Sure."

CHAPTER 23

"SURE. I DON'T SEE why not. Her family certainly seems decent enough," Miss Bitty said when Allie told her that Hannah had invited her over. "What time? I'll drive you."

"She said five."

"I have a client at five, but maybe Louis can take you. Just be in the kitchen ready to go at ten to five."

Back in her bedroom, Allie picked out an outfit to wear. Although the idea of going to Hannah's house made her nervous, it would help keep her mind off of what had happened in the garden before Hannah had arrived. Plus, the thought of actually making a friend was exciting.

She chose a pair of navy blue shorts, a black form-fitting knit top, and a pair of wedges. She washed her hair, blew it straight, and spent a lot of time with her new department store makeup, marveling at how well it went on.

An hour later, she studied the final product in the bathroom mirror. Her body was good—and looked fantastic under her new wardrobe.

As usual, though, at certain angles her face looked almost scary, even beneath the carefully applied makeup. *How I made such an ugly child is beyond me,* her mother whispered.

She shuddered—and for about the millionth time in her life, wished she could transfer a little of her body's perfection to her face. It would certainly make life a lot easier.

"Allie?"

She startled. *Not again.*

She whirled around, but it was just Miss Bitty.

"Oh God. You scared the shi—" Allie caught herself. "The *crap* out of me," she finished, her pulse racing.

"Sorry, girlie, but it's ten until five. If Louis is going to take you, you'll have to leave now."

At Hannah's doorstep, Allie took a deep breath and reminded herself to act normal.

Just act like Miss Bitty and people will accept you, she told herself. Everyone loved the old woman, so maybe if she were like Miss Bitty, people would love her, too. She'd also try to be quiet. After all, she couldn't say anything stupid if she didn't talk.

Allie was still silently coaching herself when the door swung open and Hannah appeared. Allie strained to smile at the girl, but it disappeared when she noticed Hannah's frown. "What's wrong?" Allie asked.

"You're not wearing your Daisy Dukes. You don't look as country as you did this afternoon."

"My what?"

"Daisy Dukes. Isn't that what you call them here in the South? You know, your short shorts. Like these?" Hannah pointed to the jean shorts she was wearing. They were cut very short, one jagged pant leg noticeably longer than the other. Obviously she'd cut them herself.

Hannah sighed. "Oh, never mind." She glanced past Allie and

waved to Louis, who was backing out of the driveway. "Well, come on. We'll hang out in my room."

Once they reached the bedroom, Hannah flung herself on the bed. Allie stood awkwardly by the door, thinking about bolting. *Screw having a girlfriend.* She didn't want to do this anymore. Her palms were sweating and she wanted nothing more than to chase Louis down and jump back in the car with him. After all, she'd never had a real girlfriend before, and there were probably a million good reasons why.

"I'm glad you came," Hannah said, smiling. "Sit. Stay a while."

Not having the courage to escape just yet, Allie reluctantly went to a purple beanbag chair and sat.

Hannah pulled a little round lavender tin from beneath her pillow. She unscrewed the lid and revealed purple tissue paper. "Do you party?" she asked, pulling the paper to the side and revealing a variety of pills of all shapes and sizes.

Allie's stomach clenched at the memory of overdosing in the motel room. "I don't do pills."

"No? Okay, well, that's cool." Hannah picked out two pills, tossed them in her mouth, then grabbed a can of Sprite from her nightstand and washed them down. "You know, I've always wanted to be a country girl."

Country girl? "Why?"

Hannah's eyes widened with excitement. "The music videos look cool. Wearing Daisy Dukes, riding on tractors, drinking cheap beer, making out with hot boys with big trucks. Looks like a blast."

Allie had done none of those things, so she wasn't sure how to reply. Hearing the wall clock above her ticking, she tried to figure out what Bitty would say in the same situation. Apparently Hannah hadn't yet noticed she was a social misfit, and Allie didn't want her to.

Why did I think I could possibly be friends with this girl? she asked herself, wringing her hands together.

Every once in a while a MacBook on the side of Hannah's bed would make a ringing sound and Hannah would lean over and check something on the screen. "Hey, what's your Facebook?" Hannah asked, typing something on the keyboard.

Allie had heard of Facebook but wasn't sure what it was. "Facebook?"

"Yeah, Facebook." Hannah looked up. "You've got to be kidding me. You're not on Facebook?"

"No."

"I mean, who doesn't have a Facebook?" Hannah said, flopping on her stomach. "We've got to get you an account. You can find *anyone* on Facebook."

Hannah's words were slurred and practically spilling out of her mouth. Apparently whatever the pills were that she had taken were kicking in.

"So, you ever go alligator wrestling?"

The girl was definitely odd. Allie just stared at her.

Hannah knitted her beautiful brows together. "What?"

Allie shrugged. "Never heard of it."

"Wha-at? I read that it was, like, a favorite pastime of yours down here in the bayou. There are a ton of videos on YouTube."

Footsteps sounded in the hallway outside the door. Then a woman's voice. She was talking to someone and sounded angry.

A few seconds later, there were three sharp knocks at the door. "Dinner, Hannah!"

Hannah bristled and finally stopped talking. She wiped her nose with her forearm. "God, I hate her."

A pause. Then, "Did you hear me?" the woman called through the door.

"Yes, I *heard* you!" Hannah yelled.

"Well, come on then."

"She *so* gets on my nerves," Hannah muttered. "She probably doesn't even know you're here. That's how well she pays attention to my life." She reached for the tin again, drew out two more pills, and chased them with her Sprite. "I could be blowing an entire hockey team in here and she wouldn't know."

Allie stood. "Well, I should probably go."

Hannah squinted at her. "So is Miss Bitty your mother?"

"No. She's my, uh, foster mother," Allie said, the words feeling weird coming out of her mouth.

"Get out! You're an *orphan*?"

The word took Allie by surprise. But she was, wasn't she? It was the first time she had heard the word associated with her. It sounded weird. Her . . . Allie . . . an orphan. "Yeah. I guess I am."

Hannah gazed at her with those big, beautiful brown eyes.

"What?" Allie demanded.

"I know it's probably rude to ask, but what happened to your parents?"

"My father left when I was a baby, and my mother's dead. When she died, my older brother took care of me, but he ended up killing himself last year," Allie said, surprised to hear the words leave her mouth. But once they did, she instantly felt a little better. As if talking about it, just that little bit, had maybe helped.

Hannah's eyes widened. Then her mouth spread into a skeptical smile. "You're kidding, right?"

"No."

"Holy shit," Hannah said, apparently still processing everything. "Your brother killed himself?"

Allie nodded.

"Seriously. All of this is the truth?"

"Yeah."

Three more sharp knocks on the door. "Hannah, baby, are you coming?"

Hannah rolled her eyes, then looked at Allie. "Hey, want to stay for dinner?"

Allie shrugged, squirming a little on the inside. Spending time with Hannah was one thing. But she wasn't so sure it would be a good idea to meet Hannah's parents.

"Please? Pretty please?"

The girl looked so beautiful, so hopeful, and before she knew it, Allie heard herself say, "Okay."

"Oh good!" Hannah squealed. She scrambled off her bed; then she pulled at the short, uneven inseam of her shorts and grinned at Allie.

"Uh, where's your bathroom?" Allie asked.

"First door on your left. I'm going to go ahead to the table just so her head doesn't explode. Just meet me in the dining room when you get out. It's by the front door. You can't miss it."

"Okay." Allie opened the door and stepped into the hallway.

"Oh, and Allie?"

Allie turned to see a mischievous smile on Hannah's face. "Get ready for a circus."

Allie stared at choice parts of her face in Hannah's bathroom mirror. If she looked at certain features and not her face as a whole, *maybe* she looked okay. Pretty, even. Well, sorta. That is, if you didn't see her from any of her bad angles and didn't look too carefully, *and* if the lighting was decent.

She took several long, deep breaths and tried to get it together. She had just begun having a decent time with Hannah, but now the thought of meeting the girl's parents made her stomach hurt.

They wouldn't approve of her.

No one ever did.

Maybe the new clothes would help. Maybe, too, the fact that she lived with the ever-so-popular Miss Bitty would win her some points. She wanted a chance at a friend. Wanted it badly. More than she would've thought mere minutes ago. Just the little bit of acceptance she'd already gotten from Hannah had been addictive and she craved more.

She had just gotten a small taste of what Miss Bitty must feel with having so many friends . . . and so many admirers. Miss Bitty had it good. Really good.

Even more reason to be like her.

Be good, she coached herself in the mirror. *Don't say anything stupid and maybe, just maybe, they'll let you be her friend.*

With that, she pushed the door open and forced herself to walk to the dining room.

CHAPTER 24

ALLIE STEPPED INTO the family's dining room to find Hannah and her parents already sitting down. She stood in the doorway, her heart beating miles a minute.

"Ted, Claire, this is Allie," Hannah announced from her seat.

Ted stood and extended his hand. "I'm Ted, Hannah's stepfather. It's very nice of you to join us."

"Hi," Allie said, taking the man's hand, self-conscious that her palm was clammy. He was the man she'd seen working in the yard at Miss Bitty's. He was a decent-looking older man, except for the outdated feathered hair and a couple of twisted front teeth.

She noticed the handshake seemed to be lasting too long.

He quickly released his grip. "I've seen you a few times at Miss Bitty's. I help out with projects over there from time to time. Miss Bitty," he said, smiling, "she's a remarkable woman."

"Uh, yeah."

"And as Hannah so politely announced, my name is Claire," the woman said primly, her hazel eyes icy. "Now, come sit down so we can get started." She pointed to the empty space across from her.

Allie walked around the table and sat, careful to keep her spine straight and her chin high. High enough to appear confident, but not so high as to appear arrogant or anything.

She stole a quick look at Claire. She was thin. Borderline too thin, actually. So why was she seeing Miss Bitty to lose weight?

That's odd.

Her eyes flitted from Claire to Ted to Hannah. Everyone was looking at her. A knot formed in the pit of her stomach.

"Do you like Hamburger Helper, dear?" Claire asked, picking up a big yellow bowl.

Allie brought her hand to the side of her face. "Uh, sure, thanks."

The woman handed her the bowl and Allie started spooning the food onto her plate.

"Imitation mashed potatoes?" Hannah asked, her words slurring, as she held out another big bowl. "Claire uses the fake flakes. It's really tasty."

Claire shot Hannah a look. Then her cool hazel eyes returned to Allie. They probed, scrutinizing her. Surely Claire was skeptical of her being worthy enough to be friends with her daughter. To be eating Hamburger Helper at her nice dinner table.

Willing her hands not to shake, Allie took the bowl and spooned the mashed potatoes next to the pasta and meat. A panicky sensation brewed in her stomach, making it go sour.

It was past six o'clock and the light in the room was just starting to slant. It was the time of day when Allie's mood naturally darkened. The time of day she used to go searching for her brother when she was a kid. Again, she wished she hadn't come. That she was back at Miss Bitty's, where she was finally becoming comfortable.

Hannah continued. "Hamburger Helper, powdered mashed potatoes, corn from a can. Hormones, pesticides, GMOs, deadly hydrogenated oils with a side of BPA . . . all of which will probably lead to a cancer or two," Hannah said with a smirk. Her eyes flicked to Allie's. "You might want to puke after eating this."

"That's enough, Hannah," Claire snapped. She turned her attention to Allie. "Hannah's become quite the expert on nutrition lately. So much so it's very difficult to please her with normal food."

Allie nodded silently.

The woman picked up a wineglass and took a sip. "So. What do your parents do, Allie?"

Hannah dropped her fork on her plate. "Mom, I just told you not five minutes ago she doesn't have parents! Miss Bitty's her *foster* mother."

Claire shot her daughter another nasty look. "I was just making polite conversation, Hannah!"

"But that's dumb. If you already know something—"

Ted cleared his throat but said nothing.

Claire sighed. She picked up a bowl of corn and thrust it toward Allie. "Corn, dear?"

Allie shook her head.

The bowl landed back on the table with a thud.

Allie slanted a look at Ted. The man was staring at her, chewing his food. She looked away and rearranged some of the food on her plate.

Hannah's tone softened. "Am I right, Ted? Especially something like that. I mean, why bring up something so sensitive when you already know—"

Claire's eyes darted to her husband.

Ted cleared his throat again. "Hannah, sweetheart, why don't we just change the subject."

"Well, I'm so sorry to hear that," Claire said. "About you being an orphan. I really am."

Allie shifted in her seat and bit down on her bottom lip so hard she immediately tasted blood.

The room became quiet.

Sighing, Hannah pulled a couple of pills out of her pocket, stuck them in her mouth, and chased them with her glass of water.

"*What* did you just put in your mouth?" Claire demanded.

"They're aspirins. I have a headache. Can you blame me?"

"Since when does aspirin slur your speech?"

"I'm not slurring!" Hannah slurred.

Claire sighed but said nothing.

"So, Ted. Allie said she's never gone alligator wrestling. Guess it's not as popular as we thought," Hannah said.

"No? Never been?" Ted asked, wiping his mouth, his eyes on Allie again. "I'll find a place where we can watch people do it, honey. I know how much it means to you."

"I still don't understand the fascination," Claire said. "Sounds really silly if you ask me."

"No one did," Hannah retorted.

Claire's face twitched and she stood up. "Okay, I've had about as much as I can take. I'm sorry you had to see this . . . this . . ."—she motioned toward Hannah—"*circus.*" She threw her napkin on her plate. "Nice meeting you, Allie."

The woman was right. It *was* a circus. Allie never would've guessed Hannah's family was so dysfunctional just by looking at them. Somehow Hannah and her parents made Allie's little family at Miss Bitty's look more normal. It made her appreciate her situation even more.

The woman went to the doorway, then turned, her eyes blazing. "Oh, and Allie? One word of advice. I wouldn't trust my daughter if I were you. I just wouldn't."

———

Allie stepped into the cool night. Dinner had just ended and Miss Bitty was on the way to pick her up. Hannah and her mother were in the living room arguing again, so Allie had been able to slip out unnoticed.

All she wanted to do was go home and crawl under her soft, clean sheets. She felt drained.

She had cigarettes, compliments of Big Joe, whose tidy little guesthouse bedroom she'd raided earlier in the day. She reached into her pocket for a cigarette and lit it. Taking a long drag, she stared up at the pale moon, waiting for the knot in her stomach to unfurl.

As she took her second drag, she saw something move in the darkness a few yards away.

Her body grew rigid. Coughing on the acrid smoke, she took a few steps backward and prepared to run back into the house.

"Hello?" she called. "Who's there?"

Nothing at first. Then, after a long moment, a person stepped out of the shadows. He was tall, but he was backlit by the naked lightbulb hanging above the garage and she couldn't make out his features very well.

"It's just me," the person said, his voice deep but gentle. "Don't be scared."

Allie sucked in her breath as the man stepped out of the shadows. But then she realized it was just Ted, Hannah's stepfather.

"Shit! You scared the—" She stopped, gathered her breath. "You . . . *scared* . . . me," she said.

"I'm sorry. I certainly didn't mean to," he said, reaching out as if to steady her.

She pulled away from him.

He bent to pick up the cigarette she had dropped. He handed it to her. "Are you okay?"

Allie nodded. Glancing down at her cigarette, she realized it had stopped burning.

As if reading her thoughts, Ted stepped toward her with his lighter. He flicked the tab. A flame shot out of the lighter and, reluctantly, she bent toward it and lit her cigarette.

Quickly straightening again, she created as much distance between them as she could without it being too obvious. He pulled a cigarette from a pack in his shirt pocket and lit it. Then, the two smoked their cigarettes in the darkness for a couple of minutes, neither saying a word.

After a while, Ted spoke up. "Sorry for the scene at dinner tonight. That happens a lot these days between Hannah and her mother. I'm not even sure why she invited you, knowing that something like that would probably happen."

Allie remained silent. Feeling his eyes on her, she glanced at him, her expression steely. He grinned, his crooked teeth gleaming in the darkness.

Allie didn't trust his smile. But then again, she wasn't very trusting of any man these days.

The ember from Ted's cigarette glowed in the darkness as he dragged long and hard. Several seconds later, he spoke, his voice gruff. "You know, if I were only ten years younger, I—"

Her mind flashed to the way he stared at her during dinner . . . and the memory of the truck driver who had tried to rape her . . . and of all the older men over the years who had mistreated her and asked her to do dirty things to them. Just the thought of a man, especially an older one, touching her again turned her stomach. She felt an unexpected burst of anger. "Yeah? Well, you'd still be freakin' ancient."

Ted looked confused for a moment, then he grinned. "Darling, I was just going to say that if I were ten years younger, I'd wrestle an alligator for Hannah. She's been talking about it nonstop. I think it's a strange fascination, but I'd like to see her happy again. She's been through a lot lately with the move. It's really taken its toll on her."

"Oh. Sorry. I thought—"

His face stretched into a smile. "No, I'm happily married."

Really? He calls that happy?

"And besides, you're just a kid."

Humiliated, Allie said nothing. Headlights appeared from around the corner. It was Miss Bitty.

Thank God.

"Okay, I'm going to go now," she mumbled, tossing her cigarette to the cement and grinding it out with her shoe.

"Nice to meet you, Allie," Ted said, turning to watch Bitty pull up the drive.

In the darkness Allie thought she saw him grin again. It was probably his way of laughing at her.

So much for making a good impression.

She rushed to Miss Bitty's car.

CHAPTER 25

BACK AT HOME, Allie washed up, then eagerly slipped into her nice, clean bed.

A heavy rain drummed against her window, almost immediately lulling her into a deep sleep—and a nightmare of an especially frightening summer afternoon when she had been seven years old. It was the day her mother had killed a woman Allie had really liked: Norah Duvall, a young, aspiring writer.

Norah, in the middle of writing a mystery about a small-town prostitute, had taken an interest in Allie's mother and interviewed her several times that summer for research to see how a real prostitute lived. The woman would visit the house with food (and also a little cash) and talk with her mother, sometimes recording their interviews with a cassette player.

Allie often hovered in a dark corner of the living room to study the woman while she was there, wanting to be as close as possible to her. Sometimes Norah would catch her watching and Allie would frown and look away. She was afraid that if she were nice to the writer, her mother would get angry and send one—or both of them—away. Her mother didn't approve of her being nice to people. She wanted her to be cynical and mean-spirited, just like she was.

But Allie looked forward to the woman's visits, in small part because she always brought her gifts: cheap trinkets, candy bars, Beverly Cleary and Judy Blume books. But Allie mostly looked forward to the visits because she thought the woman would one day save her. When she stopped by, Allie saw concern in the woman's eyes. Concern about Allie being trapped in the hellish whorehouse that was her childhood home. Many afternoons, Allie would catch the woman staring sadly at her for beats of time, and before long she'd come to rely on that sadness to one day save both her and her brother.

But then one afternoon something went very wrong.

The afternoon had started like most of the others. Norah had stopped by and given Allie's mother a paper grocery bag full of food. She also handed her an envelope with four twenty-dollar bills in it. Allie specifically remembered the amount because her mother had made a big production of counting the bills before stuffing them back into the envelope. Then, seeming satisfied, she started humming as she carried the food into the kitchen and poured two whiskeys.

As her mother busied herself in the adjoining room, Norah quietly handed Allie a new book, a chocolate bar, and a folded-up five-dollar bill. Then she pressed her index finger to her lips and winked.

Delighted, Allie took the gifts and scurried into her room to put her new treasures away. She'd only been gone a few seconds when she heard her mother's voice become angry. Allie hurried into the hallway to see what was going on.

"Think you're sneaky, do you?" her mother drawled, approaching Norah. "You bring your uppity college-educated ass in here and think you're goin' to pull a fast one on me? What? You think I don't have eyes? That I'm just some uneducated backwoods hooker that don't have the good sense to see that you're up to no good?" As her mother spoke, her voice continued to rise. "Well, you're wrong on all accounts, little Miss Priss. And you just crossed the wrong hooker!"

At first Norah didn't speak. When she finally did, she said, "I don't understand, Dariah. What did I do?"

"Tell me what you gave my girl behind my back!"

"Oh. It was just a few gifts. I hope that was okay? I guess I should've asked you first—"

"*What* did you give her behind my back?" the woman roared.

"Just a book and some candy, Dariah. And five dollars so she can get herself . . . you know, a little something when you go to town."

"You meddling shit!" her mother hissed.

"What? I don't under—"

Allie rushed back into her room, shut the door, and jumped into her bed. Throwing the covers over her head, she clamped her hands against her ears and began to hum, just as Norah's screaming began.

Allie hid in her bed for hours. She stayed there the rest of the afternoon and through the night. Finally, at two o'clock in the morning, she lifted the covers and listened.

Hearing her mother's loud snoring from across the hallway, she slipped out of bed and went to her door. Then she crept to the hallway bathroom, used the toilet, and headed back to her room.

But then her curiosity got the best of her, so she tiptoed down the hallway and peered into the dark living room.

The TV, tuned in to an infomercial, pulsed with silent blue and white lights. As she stared at it, something awful filled her nostrils. It took her only a few seconds to place the odor. Her stomach clenched. It was the metallic odor of blood and pine-scented cleaning solution. She'd smelled the combination many times before.

She heard a noise behind her.

It came from the kitchen.

She turned toward the sound. Peeking around the corner, she saw that her brother was on his hands and knees. Even in the dim light, she could tell his skin was pale.

She froze as she realized what he was doing. A bucket was in front of him. He was peering down, wringing out a bloody cloth. She looked around. Blood covered the linoleum and was smeared across the back door.

Hearing her, her brother looked up, his eyes glistening and urgent. "Go back to bed, Allie," he whispered. "Hurry. You don't want her to see you right now."

Thunder boomed outside, jarring Allie from her nightmare. Her eyes popped open and she stared up at the ceiling, trying to remember where she was. As the realization sank in, her frantic heartbeat began to slow.

Turning on her side, she watched the storm as it raged outside her window and tried to push the nightmare from her mind. She wanted to focus on how much better it was at Miss Bitty's.

How different her life was now.

How much safer.

CHAPTER 26

HE TOSSED AND TURNED, listening to the storm build outside. As thunder exploded in the sky, rage built inside him.

Not killing the brunette had turned out to be a big mistake. He was foolish to think he could get by with mere stalking.

He grabbed the fork from his nightstand, then quietly went to the window and watched the storm. He raked the utensil down his scarred back in long, hard strokes, trying desperately to soothe the itch.

It was making him go mad.

Crazier than he already was.

He had been seven when his rage first became a problem. The boy on the school bus had been taunting him, as many of the students did during his school days, and he'd responded by jamming the pencil, hard, into the boy's leg. If the boy had been a girl, he probably would've driven it in even harder.

Twenty minutes later, when he and his mother were in the principal's office, his mom told him to tell the principal that he was remorseful.

But he wasn't.

So he didn't say it.

The principal stared at him, red-faced. "The wound could get infected and he could die. *Then* how would you feel?"

But he had simply shrugged and said, "I don't think I'd feel anything at all."

And he'd meant it.

Telling the truth cost him a two-week suspension, and he'd been grounded at home for a solid month: no television, no Atari gaming system, no Friday pizza night, no Saturday matinees. And, eventually, after a second altercation with a different student—this one involving a pair of freshly sharpened scissors—the principal called him a monster and expelled him from the school. That was when he realized he didn't value human life like others did.

He didn't feel for people quite like others did.

He was sick, and he knew it. He was every bit the monster his principal claimed he was all those years ago.

SHE was the only living person who knew what he had done. But she didn't even know the half of it. She only knew about two women several years ago, but there had been many more.

SHE'D loved and protected him but had also promised that if he ever did it again, it would be the last time.

SHE'D abandon him.

He shivered at the thought.

Feeling fine rivers of blood snake down his back, he blinked back angry tears and finally accepted that hunting the women wasn't going to be enough anymore. He had tried. He really had.

The pain was just too much.

CHAPTER 27

SWEAT ROLLED DOWN the hollow of his back, its salt stinging his open wounds. His body felt like a big open sore.

He'd watched the house for a few hours earlier in the day and had seen the brunette come and go, each time without her son. Now certain that she was going to be alone for the night, he was going in.

He circled the house, watching for lights, movement.

No lights were on and everything was still. He easily gained entry through the back door, then closed it softly. His gloved hand tightening on the knife, he walked through the kitchen, to the living room, then down the hallway that led to the bedrooms.

His heart hammered inside his chest. He felt so utterly alive he almost couldn't stand it. No drug in the world could ever mimic what this did for him.

He stopped to check the son's bedroom and confirmed the bed was empty; then he headed to the laundry room and opened the breaker box. After flipping all the switches to the off position, he went to the front door, unlocked it, and eased it open a few inches.

Now . . . I am ready.

He moved back down the hall and assumed his place.

His blood flooded with the thrill of anticipation as he rapped hard on the wall outside of her bedroom door.

He quickly stepped into the room next to hers and listened in the darkness, hearing her stir on the other side of the wall. A few seconds later, she approached her bedroom door and flipped the light switch.

Nothing happened.

"Justin, was that you?" she called, her voice thick with sleep. "Justin? Baby, are you here?"

She swung the door open and walked down the hallway, her steps cautious, timid. He followed her, staying several paces behind. She poked her head in her son's room and tried to switch his overhead light on. "Justin?"

But of course there was no answer. And no light.

"Shit," she said, and proceeded to the living room and noticed the front door ajar and streetlight filtering in. "What the hell?"

She hesitated, staring at it for a moment. Then she hurried to the door and closed it. All was silent in the house except for the sound of the front door's dead bolt being engaged, the chain lock being put into place, and the thundering of his heart.

As she hurried toward the hallway again, no doubt heading for her cell phone, he flipped his flashlight on and aimed the beam directly at her face.

For a quick second she looked stunned, her dark eyes wide. Then she gasped and ran for the hallway. Blinded by the bright light, she misjudged her path and banged into the coffee table. She shrieked, but he clamped a hand tightly against her mouth and lifted her off the ground.

She flailed and bit at his palm as he carried her into her bedroom, but he just smiled. She was no match for him. It was like a baby bird trying to fight a wolf. Besides, when hunting, his strength and pain tolerance both increased a hundredfold.

He threw her down on the bed and pinned her. Then he shone the light into her face again.

"Please, don't," she begged. She'd gone to bed with her mascara still on and it was sliding down her cheeks.

"Why are you doing this?" she cried.

He thought about the question and decided to tell her the truth. After what he was putting her through, she deserved it.

"Because nothing else makes me feel good."

Her already wide eyes widened even more.

He shined the light on himself so she could see his face. "Do you recognize me?"

She hesitated, then drew in a shaky breath. "The supermarket."

He smiled.

"I don't understand. What did I do?"

His face hardened. "You were a bitch to me," he said. "Then, you smiled."

He turned the flashlight back on her and watched her sob.

"Please . . . I'll do anything," she sobbed.

But he didn't want *anything*. He wanted this.

She became hysterical, her chest heaving in between long sobs. "Why me?" she pleaded.

His throat clenched and unclenched like a heart. "Because you're exactly the type of woman I like doing this to. You like to hurt people, so I'm going to hurt you."

The color drained from her face.

Raising the knife above his head, his body broke out in a cold sweat. He smiled at the woman. As the corners of his lips turned up, they also drew back from his teeth. In the heat of murder, he became something different.

He became something sick.

He became himself.

———

Everything else faded away as he watched the brunette go limp. He was lightheaded with pleasure, so calm he felt he was drifting into a trance.

He realized he could finally breathe freely.

The itch had finally been extinguished again.

Hopefully for a very long time.

He decided he would take his time before leaving the house. He was exhausted. He wanted to lay next to her for a while, breathe in her odor and thoroughly enjoy the peace he'd finally found.

He lay down, closed his eyes, and, before he knew it, fell into a deep, luxurious slumber.

———

At some point, he heard the voice. "Mom?" It sounded like a young boy.

Clawing out of his deep slumber, he wrenched open his eyes. He blinked the sleep away and tried to get his bearings. He was with the woman . . . and there had been a voice.

Or had there? Maybe it had been his imagina—

"Mom, what's going on? What's wrong with the lights? Hey, Mom?"

Suddenly the overhead light bathed the room in mind-bending brightness.

Where the fuck did he come from? And how the hell did he turn on that light? I flipped off the fucking—

He saw the boy standing in the entrance of the room and his heart nearly leapt out of his chest. The kid stared, quickly comprehending the scene. He fumbled for his knife, grasping it just as the kid disappeared down the hallway . . . and he tore after him.

CHAPTER 28

CASHIERING WAS MINDLESS WORK.

It was also the type of work that could make you *lose* your mind, Allie thought a few hours into her first day at Sherwood Foods. You just say hello and smile at the customers as though you were honestly happy to see them.

Then, after the greetings and fake smiles, scan the groceries, tuck the items in the bag, making sure that fragile items like eggs are secure. Announce the total, make change, tear off a receipt, and say "Good-bye, have a wonderful day!" with a big cheesy smile on your face.

Then do it all over again.

And again.

And again.

The work in and of itself was fine. It was so easy, Allie could do it in her sleep. The difficult parts were the boredom and being in such a public place for a long period of time.

Too many people were milling around. Too many eyes were on her, watching. *Staring.* She tended to wilt under people's curious eyes. Eyes made her insecure.

As soon as Miss Bitty had dropped her off in front of the store, she knew it was a mistake. Then, when she started manning her register, she could swear the sea of customers was talking about her. Judging her. But, of course, she was just imagining it.

Well, wasn't she?

She dutifully followed her manager's commands, even though she was having a tough time concentrating with his thick hand resting on the small of her back. Many times she wanted to slap it off. To tell him what else he could do with it.

But it was important to her to do well. To make Miss Bitty proud. After all, she imagined the woman didn't have an easy time getting her the job in the first place.

At least Miss Bitty had made it a point to get her a job outside of Grand Trespass, in a place where it was less likely folks would know her and her story. Even though she had been a social hermit all her life, enmeshed with the rest of her family, chances were someone would eventually recognize her in Grand Trespass. At least here, miles outside of town, the odds were slim.

After her lunch break, someone set a few items on the conveyor belt: an egg salad sandwich, a bag of Fritos, a can of Coca-Cola. When she looked up to greet the customer, she was surprised to see Hannah's stepfather, Ted.

"I didn't realize you worked here," he said, smiling.

"I didn't. Um, well, not until today anyway," she said, remembering how much of a fool she'd made of herself the last time she'd seen him. She scanned his items quickly.

"This place is kind of out of the way, isn't it?"

She shrugged. "I guess."

"I'm building a fence for a family out here today," he said. "Figured I'd grab myself some lunch."

She rang up his last item. "Um, I guess that'll be $4.55," she said, glancing up at him. He handed her a crisp five-dollar bill. She made change and he grabbed his bag. "Well, hope to see you around the house. Hannah could use more friends."

He wants me to be Hannah's friend?

He actually approves of me?

"Uh, sure. Okay," she stammered. Maybe she'd gotten him all wrong. After all, if he approved of her, he couldn't be that bad of a guy, could he?

"Have a good day, Allie."

"You, too, Mr. Hanover," she said, and threw him a half smile.

After he walked off, someone tossed a box of powdered donuts on her conveyor belt. She looked up to greet her customer and her blood ran cold. The man glared down at her with dark, hard eyes and hissed, "How does it feel being a killer's sister?" He leaned even closer and, eyes blazing, said, "Your mama was a killer, too. Isn't that right? Both a killer *and* a whore?"

Adrenaline flooded Allie's veins. The words, said aloud and so angrily, frightened her.

"You sick, too? See, I have little kids to protect. I don't need no loony tunes working close to where they go to school and play. You follow what I'm sayin'?"

Desperate for help, Allie turned toward the automatic doors but saw that Ted was long gone. She peered up at the manager's office, but the manager wasn't there. Finally, she turned back to the man, the back of her neck on fire.

"Just so you know, I'm watching you," the man continued. "All of us are."

She heard voices close by. Looking over her shoulder, she saw a small group of teenage girls in soccer uniforms, ringed socks up to their knobby knees, staring at her from aisle eight. Five pairs of cold eyes watched her; *judged* her. She inwardly cringed, imagining what they must be thinking.

Allie turned back to the man and gripped the box of donuts so hard, the box imploded. *Do not cry . . . do not cry . . . do not cry*, she told herself, beads of sweat forming on her upper lip.

She tried to work up a fierceness in her eyes. Tried to play it tough, like she always had, but she was too scared.

Plus, the room was starting to spin.

She planted her palms against the counter in front of her just to hold herself up.

"Just know you're not wanted around here," the man said. "So you better watch your step. Don't need no copycat of what your brother did either. Sick sonofabitch."

Allie's hackles rose. Now she burned red. "My brother was ten times the man you are, you ignorant backwoods asshole!"

"No, your brother was a sick piece of shit," the man spat. "And you know what? You look like a worthless piece of shit, too."

"You don't know me."

Allie's manager appeared by her side, red-faced, confused, and smelling vaguely of liquor. "Allie? What's the matter? What's going on?"

But Allie didn't even look at him.

She was too busy working up spit in her mouth.

CHAPTER 29

BITTY DROVE ALLIE home from Sherwood Foods and, brow furrowed, silently listened to what she had to say. She didn't interrupt once. In fact, she said nothing on the drive home. Not one word.

But every time Allie glanced at the old woman, she seemed to be gripping the steering wheel even tighter.

She knew she had let the old woman down by acting the way she had, especially after Bitty had gone through the trouble to get her the job. And on her first day no less. Spitting in a customer's face. Now *that* took some serious class.

The guy in the supermarket was right: I AM a piece of shit.

Being the new and improved Allie was much more difficult than it looked. Maybe she didn't have it in her after all.

The angrier Bitty looked, the faster Allie talked, letting more and more words spill out of her mouth. She talked so quickly, she reminded herself of Hannah. For the full twenty minutes of the drive, Allie talked. She talked about what had happened at Sherwood Foods. She talked about how people never liked her. How she'd never fit in. About how crazy her mother had made her brother. About how much she missed him. About how frightened she had always been. About how difficult it was being so hideous and hated.

Most of the words tumbled out before she even knew she was going to say them. She just couldn't stand for there to be any silence between them. She was mortified that she had just lost control and screwed everything up for herself. She was trembling and desperate and felt like she had nothing more to lose—so she talked.

And Bitty listened.

Silently.

Allie was still talking when the two walked through the back door of the house.

Miss Bitty threw the car keys onto the kitchen counter and walked through the kitchen to the living room. Allie followed her, finally silent. She had run out of things to say. She also felt empty and alone. And very afraid.

"Sit," Bitty ordered. The television in the living room was tuned in to an episode of *CSI*, the blue-tinted lights flickering in the otherwise dark room. Obviously, Big Joe had left the television on. It was something she'd heard Bitty tell him not to do on at least three occasions. It was one house rule Bitty didn't bend on: wasting resources.

"That Joe," Bitty muttered, switching on a lamp. She searched for the remote control. Finding it between two couch cushions, she grabbed it, lowered the volume, then turned to Allie.

Allie sat, her throat dry. She had ruined everything. There was nothing in the world she wanted more than to live with Miss Bitty. To get tutored, get her GED, maybe go to college. To be girlfriends with Hannah. To have a chance at a real future. At happiness.

She had been wrong about the old woman. It was more than obvious that Miss Bitty was a kind person. The type her mother always told her didn't exist. The type of person people wanted to be around. The type who people respected.

Exactly the type of person Allie wanted to be, instead of who she was now: the wayward teenage tragic mess of a hooker who couldn't hold down a decent job because she didn't have the good sense not to spit in customers' faces.

"I'm so sorry," Allie said, staring down at her lap, her voice trembling.

"Oh girlie, I don't blame you a bit!"

What?

Allie's jaw dropped. For the first time since Sherwood Foods, she noticed the old woman's eyes were full of fire. They locked on hers. "Baby, you knew something like that was bound to happen once you came back here, right? I know that it didn't feel very pretty, but you have to realize that some people are just plain cruel, especially if they feel threatened." The old woman placed a soft, thin hand in hers. Allie was amazed at how paper-like the woman's skin felt.

Tears flowed from Allie's eyes. So many she couldn't wipe them all away, and some dripped into her lap.

"The only thing we can do is guard ourselves from the inside," the woman said, handing Allie a tissue.

Easier said than done. If only I knew how . . .

"I am very sorry you had to experience that. If there is one thing I have no patience for, it is bullying of any type."

"So I can stay here? Really?"

The woman's eyes softened. "Oh sweetie, of course." Miss Bitty reached out and hugged her. Allie had never been a hugger. In fact, unless it had been a sexual encounter, there'd only been a few people she'd ever touched in her whole life. But the hug felt incredible.

"You're shivering," the old woman said. She withdrew and stood up. "Go draw yourself a nice, warm bath. I'll bring you a little something to relax you. Then we can talk some more. As much as you need to, okay?"

Allie suddenly wanted to hug the old woman again, but she couldn't bring herself to reach out, so she did as Miss Bitty told her and got up from the couch. "I'll do better next time," she promised.

And she meant it.

"I will do *much* better. Just watch."

But Bitty wasn't listening to her any longer. Something on the television screen had caught her eye. The old woman picked up the remote control and turned up the volume.

The local news was showing a story. The caption SON WALKS IN DURING MOTHER'S MURDER was splashed across the bottom of the screen in large capital letters.

Allie moved to the television to get a better look. On the screen, neighbors milled about on the sidewalk in front of a ranch-style house. An attractive female reporter stood next to a tall oak tree, her hair blowing in the evening breeze. "As we reported earlier, thirty-one-year-old Lucy DeWalt, local and single mother, was stabbed thirty-two times in her home and found by her twelve-year-old son as she . . ."

Memories of the things Allie had witnessed her mother and brother do flashed in front of her eyes. Her knees went weak. "Where did that happen?" Allie whispered.

Miss Bitty spoke, quietly, without taking her eyes off the television. "Truro." Truro was three towns from Grand Trespass. It was where Sherwood Foods was located.

"Things like this don't happen here. Uh-uh. Not in this neighborhood," a heavyset woman holding a pajama-clad toddler was saying on the television. "It's really frightening. Not knowing what your neighbors are into. Makes you wonder just who people really are."

There was a sudden noise—sharp and loud—from the back of the house. Allie jumped and her nostrils filled with gunpowder.

The gunshot . . . Her brother falling to the floor.

That final night with her brother flashed in her head again, as vivid as if it were actually happening. She began to shake.

Heavy footsteps bounded swiftly toward the women. A few seconds later, Big Joe walked in with his jug of green smoothie. Seeing the women, he smiled.

Allie wanted to scream at him for continuing to open the door so loudly. For just barreling in like a bull in a china shop and nearly giving her a heart attack. He'd frightened her over a dozen of times by doing it. But she managed to bite her tongue. She was already on very rocky ground and she knew it.

"Joe, you *have* to stop doing that," Bitty snapped. "Rushing through the door like you're going to tear it down. The girl undoubtedly has post-traumatic stress syndrome, and you scare the *bejeezus* out of her every time you do that."

It was the first time Allie had seen the woman angry at someone. The first time she'd ever seen her lose her cool.

Joe's smile disappeared. "I'm sorry. I'll try to remember."

Miss Bitty's hands went to her hips. "Look, Joe. There are things we try to do and things we just do. Don't try. Do it."

"Okay."

Bitty crossed her arms. When she spoke next, her tone was softer. "I apologize for raising my voice, Joe. Please forgive me."

"No, you're fine. I'm really sorry. I'll take more care when walking into the house."

"I'd appreciate that."

Miss Bitty turned to Allie. "You're still shivering. Go take a warm bath and get some pajamas on. I'll be in soon."

A few minutes later, Allie sat in the bath with hot water trickling between her toes. She curled and straightened them under the soothing spray and tried to think of absolutely nothing, like Miss Bitty had shown her the week she'd moved in.

When a memory of the nasty words that had been said at the supermarket tried to needle its way through, she visualized a big red "Stop" sign and the thought melted away. It worked most of the time. The times it didn't, though, she found herself wanting to just disappear.

She didn't want a job anymore. Leaving the house was just too hard. Maybe she could stay home and help Miss Bitty. The woman probably could use more help—and Allie was willing to do anything she wanted her to do. *Anything* not to have to spend much time in public again. To be on display.

She stayed in the bathtub until her fingertips puckered, then climbed out and wrapped her cotton bathrobe around herself. Shuffling out of the bathroom, she found Bitty sitting on her bed, smiling.

The woman patted the down-turned bed. "Get in."

Allie crawled in and the old woman held out two pills and a glass, then set an unmarked bottle of pills on the nightstand.

"Take two of these twice a day without food and make sure to keep drinking your green drinks every morning."

"What are they?" Allie asked, taking the pills. She set down the glass of water.

"Aminos. They should help with your anxiety. And if they don't, just tell me and we'll try something different." Miss Bitty grabbed her hands again. "You're a good girl. You're nothing like what that nasty man said you are. He doesn't know you. He just knows the unspeakable things your family did."

Allie nodded.

"I also want to address something you said in the car," she continued, concern creasing her old face. "You said some really harsh things about yourself. Like how you think you're hideous and ugly, and how you just don't belong anywhere. Were you just upset, or do you really think those things?"

Allie stared at the woman. "Well, don't you?"

"Think those things?" Miss Bitty frowned. "Of course not."

"But when I got here, you said . . ."

"I said what?"

"The morning you introduced me to Joe. You said I was ugly."

The old woman looked perplexed at first, but then realization slowly crept into her eyes. "Oh Allie! That was more of a figure of speech than anything. You were behaving so rudely, so yes, I saw ugliness. I was making a point . . . and a good one." She paused and squeezed Allie's hand. "But my God, I used the wrong words and I'm so sorry. I don't, for an instant, want you to believe such things about yourself, you hear me?"

Allie was confused.

"Honestly, attitude, and behavior aside . . . if we're just talking about physical features, you're gorgeous." She took Allie's face in her hands. "I mean, look at you. You are one of the most physically attractive young women I've ever seen. It's just when you're acting ugly, your behavior overwhelms those features. Makes you much less appealing."

She's lying to you. You're hideous and you know it.

"But my mother even told me I was ugly." *Actually, she still does.*

"Oh dear. Your mother was wrong, Allie."

Tears flooded Allie's eyes. "How can you say I'm gorgeous? Seriously. How can you? It's *so* confusing!"

Miss Bitty smiled. "Because you are. But whether you are stunning or ugly as sin, what matters most is that you're pretty on the inside. And Allie, you are. And you get prettier each and every day in all of the important ways."

"How come what I see in the mirror is so ugly then?"

Miss Bitty gripped her hands again. "Well, I'm no expert, but I'm sure it has a lot to do with everything you've gone through, girlie. You've shouldered more pain in your young life than most people will ever see. You were raised by someone sick who taught you all the wrong things."

Miss Bitty's words made Allie's heart ache in a good way. She let her tears flow and didn't bother wiping them away.

But she doesn't know who you really are. The disgusting things you've done.

Allie decided to come totally clean. "I'm not who you think I am. I'm not a good person. I've only been pretending so you don't send me away," Allie admitted, the tears coming more forcefully.

"It's okay. We all find ourselves pretending sometimes."

Although the woman's words were comforting, Allie began to bawl . . . and she couldn't stop.

"I've slept with men . . . for money," she blurted out, frightened to look into Miss Bitty's eyes.

Miss Bitty reached out and squeezed her hand.

Did she not understand what I just said?

"Do you understand what I'm saying? And . . . and it was actually a lot of men. Too many to count," Allie sniffed. "I'm disgusting. I really am."

The woman embraced Allie. "No, you're not disgusting. You're just a confused young girl," she said, patting her back. "You've had a very difficult life . . . and made mistakes, but your mistakes don't define you. Lord, if they did, we would all be in a world of trouble."

Miss Bitty pulled away from Allie and stared into her eyes. "I'm so happy that you finally trust me enough to confide in me. It's good for you. It's good for us *both*."

Allie wiped her eyes, incredulous that the woman still wanted anything to do with her.

"Just continue to work on yourself, girlie. Bring out all of that inner beauty, the only beauty that ultimately matters—and know that I'm here anytime you need help. You understand?"

Allie nodded.

135

"Miss Bitty," she sniffed. "I don't want another job. I don't feel comfortable being around a lot of people. Please . . . don't make me."

"Of course. I won't make you do anything you're not comfortable with."

Allie breathed a sigh of relief.

The two sat in silence for several minutes, their fingers intertwined, until Allie was able to catch her breath again. Once she did, she realized that she felt much better; better, but exhausted.

"That's all I had to say. Would you like to talk some more about today?" Bitty asked.

"I don't think so."

"Well, if you change your mind, I'm here."

The old woman gave her hands one last squeeze, then released them and left the room.

Allie lay, staring at the ceiling, hopeful that the woman wasn't just trying to be nice. That maybe it was true and she really wasn't hideous. That maybe it was just her mind playing more tricks on her. She considered going to the mirror to look but in the end decided not to.

Feeling drowsy, she replayed how good the woman's fingers had felt laced in between her own. The feeling of skin on skin for reasons other than sex.

For the first time since Johnny left, she didn't feel so alone. Someone finally cared about her. Like, really truly cared.

She could hardly believe it. She closed her eyes and let herself drift off.

The woman is a liar. She's lying to you, the voice hissed into her ear. But Allie was too far gone to even hear it, much less let it bother her.

CHAPTER 30

HE TOOK ONE last anxious drag, then tossed his cigarette into a coffee can. Walking to the tree, he yanked hard on the rope.

Yes, the branch was still sturdy.

He stared at the knot, which, of course, was perfect. He'd made many over the years. After all, people like him, who did unspeakable things—and who would also do nothing but shrivel up and die in a prison cell—needed an exit plan. Satisfied with his handiwork, he walked to the back door.

He still couldn't believe how royally he'd fucked up. How lazy he'd gotten. He wasn't sure who he was angrier with: himself for being so stupid or the son for screwing everything up.

Once inside, he turned on the television and instantly found what he was looking for. Front and center on the six o'clock news.

The lead story.

Shit.

He had hoped it would get very little coverage. After all, the country was at war. People died *every day*. And this one woman had been truly meaningful to who? Maybe *five* people . . . if she was lucky?

But, of course, the local news would jump on it. And people would talk. He'd only been fooling himself. It was small-town Louisiana, after all.

Feeling a muscle in his cheek jump, he angrily watched. According to the reporter, the woman's son and a friend had returned to the house and had found the power out. The friend had then gone to check the breaker box while the boy went to check on his mother. That's when he caught the murderer in his mother's room. The boy ran and the suspect pursued the child through the woods, but the boy was able to get away.

There had been two boys.

Now it made sense. The question now was, did either boy get a good enough look at him to describe him?

Feeling his face redden, he recounted the events of that night. He had run after the son but hadn't been quick enough. He had burst through the hallway and rounded the corner of the living room just in time to see the kid flee through the back door, then fly into the woods out back. He chased him into the woods but almost instantly lost his trail.

At that point, he gave up and scrambled back to his car.

He wondered where the other kid had been . . . if he'd been watching him the entire time.

He shivered at the thought.

He tried to imagine what people would say about him if he got caught. Cable television was now riddled with true crime shows. Shows featuring killers much like him. Fathers, sons, brothers, athletes, military leaders, the perpetually reserved, the flamboyant. These were people who had the same types of urges as he did. People who didn't know any other way to quiet those urges. People who fit perfectly into their communities until they were found out.

Inconsequential people were often interviewed on the news networks. "I always kept my eye on that one," a lot of them would say. But in actuality, they probably never kept an eye on him. Never even noticed him that much, really. People didn't notice much at all these days. They were too occupied with themselves.

The reporter's next words chilled him to the bone: "The sheriff's department says a composite sketch of the suspect is under way . . ."

His blood ran cold. He gripped the armchair.

CHAPTER 31

SHE STOOD IN front of him, her eyes icy. Like everyone else in town, she'd seen the news reports. She wanted to know if he had anything to do with the woman's murder.

"Of course not," he lied.

She studied him, weighing his words.

"Look, I wouldn't have much respect for myself if I were to start lying to you again. So trust me, okay?" He said the next three words very slowly, his eyes wide for emphasis. "I'm . . . not . . . lying."

Her eyes grew small as she appraised him. He saw her analyze his jugular—to see if it was pumping harder than usual. She was searching for any telltale sign of deceit she could find.

Unfortunately, she'd had years of practice.

He tried to mask his anger. "But having said that, if you feel the need to know where I am 24/7, then fine. I'll tell you," he said with a sigh, hoping to make her feel ridiculous so she would say no. "Really. Is that what you want? Is that how you want us to be?"

She said nothing, but he did notice her eyes soften. She was falling for it . . . again.

"Look, we've come so far. Please . . . don't doubt me now. I love you. I would never do those bad things again. It was someone else. Some small-town crazy. Not me."

He could see her hackles lowering. His claims were soothing her. He knew she wanted badly to believe him—and he used it for leverage. It was a skill he'd learned well over the years.

The fine art of deception.

He folded her into his arms and held her, breathing in the clean scent of her hair before she finally broke away from him. Then, appearing somewhat satisfied, she finally turned on her heel and walked away.

Relieved, he watched her go.

She believed him. What she didn't know was that no matter what he did, she still would. No matter how suspicious she became or how much they argued, she just didn't know how not to.

He had always hated her for judging him. For always having to worry about what she'd think before making a decision. Fortunately, though, every time he hunted successfully his anger toward her dulled, making the relationship manageable. Most times even enjoyable. He didn't want to be angry with her because she was the only person who had ever believed in him. The only person who had never let him down.

The problem was, she didn't understand a very big part of him. Not that he expected her to. He didn't understand it himself.

All that he knew for certain was that hunting wasn't a choice. It was survival.

CHAPTER 32

LOUIS SANK BACK in his chair and cradled his coffee mug between his hands. "Miss Bitty told me what happened at the supermarket. I'm really sorry."

Allie kept her eyes trained on the science handouts Louis had given her. She didn't want him to see that her face was red.

What exactly did Miss Bitty tell him?

Hopefully not the part about the man calling her a piece of shit. She didn't want him to know that. Louis thought she was smart and treated her like she was someone worthwhile, someone important even. She didn't want him to change his opinion of her. Because if he did, she was afraid she just might, too.

"Do you want to talk about it? About what happened at the supermarket?"

"No."

Realizing that Louis could see one of her bad angles, she turned her head to the window and readjusted her chair.

That morning when she woke up, the first thought that popped into her head was Miss Bitty's words the evening before. How she had told her that she was attractive.

Gorgeous even.

Hoping she'd magically see something different than what she'd always seen before, she had hurried to the mirror only to be disappointed. She looked the same as always. Borderline scary. So, as far as her looks were concerned, she was as confused as ever.

Louis cleared his throat and laced his fingers above his head. "Allie, can I ask you a question?"

"Yeah."

"Is there a reason why you always do that with your face?"

Allie felt her face redden again.

"What?"

"The way you hide it. Cover it sometimes with your hair. You do it a lot with your hand, too. Do you feel as though you need to hide something?"

"What are you talking about?" she asked, her tone incredulous, as though she had no clue what he was talking about. She shot him a dirty look and shifted in her seat (to perfect the new angle), then tucked her hair behind her ear.

"Are you ashamed of something?"

Yes . . . of SO many things. "No. Why?" she challenged. "Should I be?"

"I'm just saying that you're a beautiful girl. But even if you weren't, there would be no reason to hide yourself."

There's that word again: beautiful. WHAT are these people seeing that I am not?

"But I'm not hiding."

"Okay, if you say so," Louis said, rising. He went to the bank of windows.

Allie watched him open a window and noticed a man in the yard hauling wood. She looked more closely and realized it was Hannah's stepfather, Ted. She kept her eyes on the man until he disappeared around the back of the house. "What's Mr. Hanover doing here?"

"Miss Bitty hired him to build the new chicken coop."

"Chicken coop? We're getting chickens?"

"I would assume so if you're getting a coop," Louis said with a wink.

The mudroom door opened and closed, then Ted poked his head into the kitchen. "I hope I'm not interrupting anything. Miss Bitty said I could come in and get some sweet tea."

"No, that's fine. Help yourself," Louis said. "We were just wrapping up anyway. Starting the coop today?"

"Yep. Hopefully it'll be done by tomorrow evening. Then I can get started on the additions to the guesthouse." Ted's eyes flickered to Allie. He looked away without saying a word.

Allie frowned. He had been so nice to her at Sherwood Foods. Maybe he was just uncomfortable about the embarrassing conversation they'd had at his house. Maybe he thought she told Miss Bitty or Louis about it?

She watched the man pour his tea and disappear outside.

"Is there anything you want to share with me before I go?" Louis asked. "I want to listen if you do."

"No."

"Alright then." Louis rose and began packing up. "Have your English and science reading done before our session Monday morning, okay?"

"Yeah," she said, staring out the window.

Louis zipped up his backpack and hoisted it onto his shoulder. "Okay, my smart girl. I'll see you on Monday. Have a great weekend."

There was that word again. Smart. Allie got butterflies in her chest.

A few minutes after Louis left, as she was basking in the glow of his words, the door to the mudroom swung open again.

This time it was Miss Bitty who poked her head in.

"Got a surprise for you, girlie," she announced with a big smile. "Come out and see."

CHAPTER 33

THE OLD WOMAN'S eyes were bright. "So what do you think? Ever have a puppy before?"

"Uh, not really," Allie lied, staring at the little red puppy that was squatting in the yard.

"Well then, it's about time you did," Miss Bitty said, smiling broadly. "Every young lady should have a dog."

Allie frowned. "What? It's . . . it's mine?"

"Yep. She's all yours!"

Allie wasn't sure what to say. Just looking at the thing brought back horrible memories. But she didn't want to be rude. Not after everything the old woman had done for her.

"Thank you," Allie said, crossing her arms and wondering what the hell she was going to do with it.

Bitty squatted down to pet her. "Isn't she cute?"

Allie smiled weakly.

"I saw the poor thing barely dodge a truck on Main Street. When I stopped to get her, I saw that there was one that looked just like her dead in the ditch. A little male puppy. Poor thing never had a chance."

The puppy wobbled toward her, sniffing. She was an odd-looking little thing. Her legs were too long for her body. Her head seemed too large. Her disheveled fur was an unmanageable frizzy mess.

"Well, I better get back inside. I have chores to do," Allie murmured.

Bitty waved her off. "The chores can wait. You two hang out . . . get acquainted."

A few minutes later, Allie sat cross-legged on her bed, staring at the puppy as she wobbled around, sniffing everything. She had just devoured two large bowls of chicken and rice and lapped up half a bowl of water. She glanced up at Allie, her muzzle wet.

When Allie looked at the puppy, she couldn't help but think of Petey, a stray dog she'd had when she was about eight years old. She'd found Petey roaming around their pond out back, took him in, and had instantly become attached to him.

She'd had Petey for about a month when her mother had taken an interest in the animal. Allie'd been napping in her room, with the dog at the foot of her bed.

"Petey! C'mon, boy. I have a nice, meaty bone for ya," her mother had said, her tone strangely upbeat.

At that point, Allie had learned to avoid her mother at all costs, so she pretended she was sleeping, but her heart pinched thinking that her dog would be anywhere near her mother. She knew the woman was up to something and that it wasn't going to be good.

The dog had been hesitant, too.

"C'mon, sweet doggy," the woman continued to coax.

The dog growled in protest and the woman rushed toward him, hooked a rope around his neck, and yanked him out of the room.

A moment later, the screen door to the back of the house screamed open and snapped shut.

Tears in her eyes, Allie jumped out of her bed and went to the window to find her mother dragging a bucking Petey into the woods.

Now bawling, Allie hurried from the room and followed them through the woods at a safe distance. When she returned home, she spent the rest of the day crying under her blankets.

Later that evening she heard her mother screaming at her brother. Blaming him for what had become of the dog. The woman told him that he was a sick son of a bitch to have done what he did.

Her brother had claimed he didn't know anything about it, which he didn't. That night he got a good beating, and Allie lay huddled in her bed, trying to block out his screams and the images she'd seen earlier in the day.

Emerging from her memory, she realized the puppy was sitting in front of her, staring. The puppy let out a shrill, demanding bark, but Allie just watched her, not sure what she wanted.

The puppy barked again, louder.

She frowned. "What the hell do you want?"

The pup retracted from Allie as though Allie'd hit her. She sat on her haunches and whimpered. She was scared.

Reluctantly, Allie reached down and scooped the pup up. She peered into the puppy's big blue eyes. "I have no idea what to even do with you."

The dog stared back and snorted.

Allie pulled the dog away from her face. "I'm not in the market to get close to anything else right now. I'm taking a big chance with the old lady as it is."

The pup snorted again, then whipped out her tongue and licked Allie's cheek.

"Eww, gross!" Allie said, distancing her face from the animal even more. The pup continued to stare at her, but now she looked as though she was smiling.

Allie found herself smiling, too. "Crap. Okay," she whispered, "but it *better* be safe to like you, you hear me?"

The pup's tail beat furiously against her and she licked her again, making Allie feel warm inside. Then, Allie heard a whooshing sound and her leg began to feel warm, too.

"No, no, don't *pee* on me!"

That night she lay in bed with the pup, watching her gnaw on a piece of knotted rope Miss Bitty had made for her. Every once in a while, the pup would stop and snort, reminding her of a pig.

"You sure do snort a lot," she said.

The pup cocked its head and stared at her. Then she snorted again.

"I think I'm going to call you Piglet."

She yipped and wagged her tail hard.

"You like that name?"

The puppy thumped her tail against the bed.

"And you like me, too, don't you?"

The puppy let out another yip, then went back to gnawing on her rope.

Allie watched the puppy, her heart swelling. Miss Bitty had been right. She really *was* cute. "How could anyone in their right mind abandon you? Just leave you to die?"

She reached for the small dog and scratched behind her ears. The puppy leaned into her fingers, her tail thumping hard against the bed.

"You know, I lost my brother, too. It's hard, but you'll be okay. I think we both will."

Piglet gazed into her eyes.

"I'm going to take really good care of you, li'l lady. Just you watch and see. Maybe I couldn't help Petey, but I'll help you."

In bed that night, listening to "Lay, Lady, Lay," Allie cradled a snoring Piglet in her arms. She slept peacefully, comforted by the puppy's warm little body.

But in the wee hours of the night, her eyes fluttered open, and she thought she noticed the outline of someone standing in the doorway. She immediately squeezed her eyes closed. *Whoever, or whatever, the hell you are, you are NOT going to ruin my brand-new life,* she told herself.

Then she willed herself to fall asleep.

CHAPTER 34

AUTUMN ARRIVED, BRINGING orange leaves, crisp breezes, and inevitable . . . unwanted . . . change.

During the daytime hours, Bitty kept Allie busy with food preparation, cleaning, and client paperwork. Allie also took some of Miss Bitty's self-care classes and learned cleansing practices like oil pulling, dry brushing, and meditation.

With Miss Bitty and Louis's help, Allie felt better than she'd ever felt. More whole, certain of herself, and, best of all, she had finally convinced herself she was someone worthwhile.

Who cared how she looked, right? These days she spent as little time as possible in front of the mirror. Instead, she concentrated on other, more important, things.

Things she had some control over.

She was starting to finally feel some inner peace—and, for the first time, didn't mind being alone very much, especially if she was with Piglet, which she nearly always was. The pup had become her sidekick—and the pup loved her unconditionally.

Over the weeks, Allie carefully studied how Miss Bitty interacted with everyone: with Big Joe, with Louis, with her various clients. Even with the guy who brought the gallon-sized bottles of filtered water and always asked for free nutrition advice. She found Miss Bitty was nice to everyone, no matter who they were, or what she could gain from them. She was the stark opposite of Allie's mother in every way.

Everyone Miss Bitty met seemed to become family. They wanted to hang around, to linger. They wanted to bask in the woman's energy because it was so good.

Miss Bitty was a healthy person, and she validated Allie. Allie now realized that validation was one of the things she'd always wanted from her brother but had never gotten. It was part of what had made her so angry with him. But it hadn't been his fault. He'd been very sick. He'd had enough trouble taking care of his own self, much less been able to attend to Allie's every need.

Allie only saw Hannah sporadically, whenever the girl wasn't busy, which wasn't very often. Hannah had made friends at school and joined the soccer team—which left little time for Allie. But it didn't bother Allie much because she was genuinely enjoying her time with everyone at Miss Bitty's.

At night, she and Miss Bitty would lie on the couch together and watch what the old woman called junk television: syndicated sitcoms or reality programming. Sometimes Big Joe or Louis would join them, but mostly they spent the time alone. It had become a comforting ritual Allie looked forward to.

Allie realized most teens would probably find her life boring, but she didn't. Feeling safe and wanted trumped excitement by a landslide. Besides, she was working on herself. With Miss Bitty's help she was becoming different; better.

People were actually going to like her now.

She no longer was the pariah she'd always been.

She was working hard on becoming the new Allie and, despite a few minor slipups, she was doing a good job. She was even starting to like the person she was becoming.

There was only one thing that cast a long shadow on all of the good. It was something that Allie had tried so hard to ignore, to compartmentalize and shove to the back of her mind. But it was no longer working. She needed to talk to someone about what she was hearing and seeing.

She needed some help.

———

Allie stepped barefoot onto the cool porch of the guesthouse.

"That wouldn't be contraband, would it?" she asked, using a word Miss Bitty used often.

Big Joe glanced at her from where he sat. He was smoking a cigarette, and an empty gallon of what had been a green smoothie was next to him. And next to that, a bottle of whiskey.

Miss Bitty was at a conference in Dallas and would be gone all day. Before the old woman left, she'd instructed Allie to stay in the house with the doors locked. The only exception, she said, was when she needed to let Piglet out.

She wasn't to open the door for anyone. And Allie had followed the old woman's rules all day. She completed the homework Louis had assigned. She even worked ahead of the curriculum and read three extra chapters in her science text. But now the house felt awfully empty, and she was lonely. Plus, she had a question she was desperate to ask someone. It was something that had been bothering her a lot lately.

Venturing outside, it took her all of ten seconds to find Big Joe sitting on the guesthouse porch, doing things he wouldn't normally be doing had Miss Bitty been around. "Bitty asked me to keep an eye on you while she was gone," Joe said. "I was just about to check on you."

"Yeah?" Allie grinned. "Before or after you got drunk?"

"Heh."

Allie set Piglet down to roam in the grass. "Anyway, I can keep an eye on myself."

"Not sure how you can manage that. At least physically," he said, then took a long drag off his cigarette.

Good one. The big man is actually clever.

"She told me not to open the door for anyone, so how were you supposed to keep an eye on me?"

"She wanted me to call you."

"Oh."

Allie studied the man for the first time in weeks. He looked different. Slimmer. Much less bloated. She lowered herself to the opposite side of the porch and contemplated asking him her question.

The two grew silent. Allie knew now was the perfect time to ask, but she was a little afraid.

A gust of wind sent bed linens fluttering on the clothesline a few yards away. Joe dragged on his cigarette, then stared off into the woods. "So what's the deal with the sheriff coming around yesterday?" he asked, flicking some ash into a cup.

"Just asking more of their same stupid questions," Allie said. She dug some dirt from the ground with her bare toe. She was sick of the sheriff and the FBI agent's visits. Her brother was dead, so even if she wanted to give them information, which she didn't, it was all pretty much pointless anyway.

"Questions about what?"

Allie narrowed her eyes and stared at him. "You don't know?"

"No. Why? Should I?"

Allie shrugged. "They're just asking questions about my brother and the murders. I guess they think I know something I'm not telling them. Either that or they have nothing else to do."

Big Joe looked incredulous. "Brother? Murders?"

Allie realized that he didn't know. She'd just assumed he did, but with him being from out of town, she supposed it made perfect sense that he didn't.

"Yeah. My brother killed two teenagers last year. But he died, so I don't know why they still care so much. They say they're just wrapping up loose ends, but they could just be saying that. I really don't know."

"He killed people? You've got to be kidding me."

She wished she were kidding. Piglet let out a few yaps, then bounded out from around the house. The pup came to a stop a few feet in front of the two, then poked her head in a bush.

"I didn't know that. I'm really sorry, Allie."

Allie watched Piglet disappear around the corner of the guesthouse and thought about her question.

"Why did he do it?" Joe asked, his voice almost a whisper.

Allie didn't want to answer any more questions. From the law, from Big Joe . . . from anyone. "I don't want to talk about it."

"Okay. I understand."

Allie listened to the crickets chirping as she watched the puppy root around. She wrapped her arms around her middle and realized she was getting tired. She thought about the comfortable bed awaiting her in the main house.

"Looks like it might storm again. I swear, in all my years, I've never seen such bad weather," Joe said, peering at the sky.

It *had* been unseasonably rainy. But Allie was used to storms. Gazing at the dark sky, she wondered how she could ask Big Joe her question without sending up any red flags. She'd just be casual about it . . . although it really wasn't a casual subject. What she needed to know is how uncommon (or common) it was to hear things, and see things from time to time. Things that weren't actually there although they sounded and looked as real as anything else.

Maybe if it happened to others—people who seemed totally normal—she was normal, too. She needed to hear that she wasn't being haunted. But more importantly, she wanted to rest assured that she wasn't losing her mind, and for now, talking to Miss Bitty about it wasn't an option. She wanted the old lady to be proud of her. Not worried that she had a head case on her hands.

The longer she procrastinated about asking him, the more exhausted she felt.

"You look tired," Joe said.

"I am," she said, deciding it was a bad idea after all. She called for Piglet and scooped the puppy into her arms.

"C'mon. Let me walk you inside."

"You're not supposed to be in the house at night when Miss Bitty isn't here. Remember?"

"Well, what she doesn't know won't exactly hurt her, will it?" Joe smiled. "Let me walk you."

Once inside the main house, Allie and Big Joe walked down the hallway that led to the bedrooms.

"Hey, I'm really sorry about the slamming-the-door-open thing," he said. "I didn't mean anything by it. I've just had a lot on my mind lately and I wasn't thinking. It's easy for me to be that 'bull in the china shop' kinda guy if I'm not careful."

Allie opened her bedroom door and deposited Piglet, who happily bounded inside. "Apology accepted," she said. Then a crazy thought popped into her head. "But there *is* a way you could make it up to me if you really wanted to."

CHAPTER 35

BITTY'S BIG PLAN was unraveling . . . fast.

After learning about the murder, she knew that everything she had set into motion would need to come to a grinding halt.

The girl's trust in her had grown immensely, so much so that Bitty had been ready to move to phase two of her plan. But now that would have to wait.

She lowered her windows and the car filled with cool, evening air as she sped out of downtown Dallas toward I-20 and Grand Trespass. She was heading home from a conference, an obligation she would've canceled if she could have, but it had been planned far in advance and too many people had been counting on her. She had asked the girl to come with her, but crowds made her nervous, so she let her stay home under a few conditions.

After learning about the murder, she hadn't felt comfortable leaving Allie alone for very long—much less an entire day. Making matters worse, she'd tried calling. But no one had answered. She berated herself again for a lifetime of mistakes. This being just one of so very many.

The depression Miss Bitty had battled over the years was also descending upon her again, making everything hopelessly murky, making her question her instincts.

During the conference, she had intuited that something horrible was going to happen again. She cursed her ability for the millionth time. It gave her just enough warning to cause her to worry. But rarely was there enough information to be helpful so she could put a stop to whatever it was that was going to happen.

Her eyes burning with tears of frustration, Miss Bitty floored the accelerator, sending her car thundering toward Grand Trespass.

CHAPTER 36

ALLIE LAY UNDER the covers with Piglet and switched Joe's iPad on.

Since Hannah had mentioned Facebook, she had been dying to check it out and see if Johnny was on it. There hadn't been many days since the morning he split on her in the motel room that she hadn't thought of him.

Had she really fallen in love with him? Would he fall in love with her if he had the chance to see how much different—*better*—she was becoming?

About a week before he left, Allie had found one of his credit cards on the motel room floor. Without giving it much thought, she had hidden it in her bag just to have something of his. She looked at the card now to double-check the spelling of his last name.

She powered on the iPad, navigated to Facebook, and found the "Search" bar. She typed in "Johnny Girard."

Several listings came up. She scrolled through the different thumbnail-sized profile photos until she finally found one that looked like him. Bursting with anticipation, she clicked on it and the photo grew larger.

Yes—it's him! It's Johnny!

She clicked on an album containing seventy-six photos, but the site wouldn't let her access it because she wasn't a friend of his.

She frowned—and her frown grew deeper when she saw that next to his relationship status, it said "It's Complicated." Did he have a girlfriend? And if so, when had that happened?

Before or after me?

She scanned the rest of his information and nearly gasped when she noticed it said he lived in Dallas, Texas.

But Johnny had told her he lived in California?

She clicked the word "Message" and typed:

Hey, it's Allie!
Remember me?
Found your credit card on the floor of the motel room
after you left. Maybe I can mail it to you or something?

Later,
Allie

Her finger hovered over the "Send" button for several minutes as she read and reread the message to see if it sounded casual enough. Finally deciding it was okay, she sent it.

A few minutes later, Allie powered the iPad off and, in the darkness, set it on the bedside table. Piglet shifted, her little paws scrabbling lightly against Allie's stomach. She repositioned the pup and pulled the covers up to her neck. Yawning, she glimpsed something blocking the light from the hallway that squeezed through the narrow crack beneath the door.

She frowned. "Joe?"

Silence.

"Joe, is that you?"

Again, no answer.

Her body tense, she stared at the door.

From beneath the covers, the puppy emitted a low, long growl, and whoever—*or whatever*—it was went away.

CHAPTER 37

THE EXTERIOR LIGHTS to the ranch house were burning when Bitty finally pulled into the drive. It was well into the morning hours and if it weren't for the adrenaline still throbbing in her old veins, she would have been exhausted.

Unlocking the back door, she hurried into the house and headed straight to Allie's room. She eased the door open, blinked, and let her eyes adjust. Then she saw her.

Buried beneath the covers with just a slender arm hanging out. She waited for some movement. Any at all, to set her mind at ease. Piglet's small head popped out from the comforter and the dog emitted a low growl, which pleased Bitty. It was exactly why she'd wanted Allie to have the little dog.

For protection.

Allie mumbled something in her sleep and turned over.

Thank you, God. She's okay.

Safe and sound in her bed. Exactly where she should be.

With a sigh of relief, Bitty closed the door and headed to the kitchen to uncork a bottle of wine.

CHAPTER 38

"I IMAGINE IN a few weeks, you'll be more than ready to ace your GED," Louis said, cleaning his glasses.

Allie and Louis were sitting at the patio table on the deck. They'd just finished some reading comprehension. Allie had passed everything with flying colors.

Louis sat back in his chair and laced his fingers over his head. "After you get your GED, Miss Bitty wants us to work on some practical stuff, like personal finance and sharpening your interpersonal skills. We'll also look into courses at Truro Community College for the spring semester. How's all that sound?"

Freaking awesome! "It sounds fine."

Louis grinned. "Just fine? Really?"

Allie felt her lips turn up at the corners.

"Yeah. That's what I thought."

Me? College? Really? Who would've ever thought?

Allie's eyes wandered to Ted and Miss Bitty, who were a few yards away, discussing the additions to the guesthouse. Allie watched Ted, as he gestured at the building with his hands. Miss Bitty seemed to be listening to what he had to say, then she walked into the guesthouse. Ted turned and his eyes locked on hers.

Allie quickly looked away.

"What's wrong?" Louis asked, glancing from Allie to Ted.

"Huh? Nothing. Why?"

Louis's eyes lingered on Ted, who was now walking around the side of the guesthouse, staring at the roof. "Well, I just saw the way you looked at him," he said, frowning. "You looked . . . upset."

Not upset. Confused. I just wish I knew whether he liked me or not. Approved of me being friends with Hannah. "Really. I have no idea what you're talking about."

"Does Ted make you uncomfortable?"

"No."

"Would you tell me if he did?"

Allie realized she had no idea. *Would* she feel comfortable enough to go to Louis?

"Allie, you're a beautiful young woman—and Miss Bitty's job is to protect you. And I'm not saying Ted would do anything inappropriate, I'm not saying that at all because he seems to be a very nice guy, but sometimes beauty makes men do things they shouldn't do. So if he makes an advance on you, or in any way makes you uncomfortable, you need to tell either Miss Bitty or me. Do you understand me?"

Louis thinks I'm beautiful?

"Allie?"

"Sure."

"Sure what?"

"I would tell one of you guys."

Louis stared at the guesthouse for a moment, then drained his coffee and set his mug down. "You're a smart girl, but you're still very young."

Beautiful. Smart. Allie tried on the images in her head—and felt like she'd swallowed a flutter of butterflies again.

She loved how Louis saw her. How Miss Bitty saw her. Even Big Joe and Hannah. They all treated her with respect. They all thought she was worthwhile. Through their eyes, she was beginning to see herself much differently.

"I'm just saying that if you need help with something, or just need to talk about something you don't understand, you should."

Something dark passed through her mind's eye. Louis was right. Even though things were going great, there *were* things bothering her. Things she wanted to talk about. Things that had absolutely nothing to do with Ted. She just didn't know where to start.

"Allie? Did you hear me?"

"Uh, okay."

"Does that mean you're listening to what I'm saying?"

Allie met Louis's eyes and held them; eye contact was one of the things she was getting much better at these days. "Yes, I heard you."

"Is there anything you want to share with me before I go? I want to listen if you do."

Yes. I'm hearing voices and I'm seeing things. And it's starting to scare the shit out of me. I really need to talk to someone about it, but I'm too scared to.

Allie willed her mouth to open. To just spit it out. But nothing happened. She was too afraid to say anything, because she felt that if she did, it would make it more real. Plus, Louis might not have such a high opinion of her any longer. He would probably think she was crazy.

"Allie?"

"No."

"You sure?"

"I'm sure."

Louis sighed. "Okay then."

He stood. "Oh, I almost forgot. I've got a little surprise for you." He pulled a handful of books out of his backpack. "I know you don't like to go out much, so I checked these out for you at the library."

Allie took the books. Three young adult books that looked like an adventure trilogy of some type.

A thrill shot through her chest at just holding them. For their curriculum she'd only read classics like *To Kill a Mockingbird* and *Jane Eyre*, which were good, but this would purely be pleasure reading.

"Just let me know when you're done with these and I'll return them and get you some more if you'd like."

Allie had the urge to jump up and hug Louis for his thoughtfulness. But, of course, she didn't.

"Thank you."

"You're very welcome," he said and began packing his backpack. "Well, you did a fantastic job this morning. Have a great day and make sure to have your homework completed by Friday."

"Okay." She beamed. "I will."

CHAPTER 39

JEALOUSY SOURED ALLIE'S mood as she watched Hannah interact with the others across the dining room table.

After not hearing from the girl for weeks, Hannah had somehow weaseled her way into an invitation to not only eat dinner at Miss Bitty's but also stay the night.

At first, Allie wasn't so sure she wanted her at Miss Bitty's house at all. And now that she was there, she was *certain* she didn't want her there, because as soon as she'd arrived, it seemed like Allie had become invisible. The girl had it all: beauty, charm, great social skills. She had it so easy.

Too easy.

Yes, maybe most of the males over the age of twelve who Allie had encountered since she was thirteen years old had shown signs of being attracted to her in one way or another. Perhaps Miss Bitty was right and she was more attractive than she thought, because her looks had always gotten her male attention. It didn't matter who the guys were: single, in a committed relationship, married, divorced, widowed, if they were fathers, grandfathers, Bible thumpers or atheists. She always noticed the lingering looks, the double- and triple-takes. Some didn't bother to hide it. Some tried unsuccessfully. They flirted, ogled, and, in the last couple of years, many had even paid for dates.

But Hannah was a different creature altogether. First of all, she didn't have to work hard at concealing anything or faking it. Hannah was the real thing. And it didn't take a rocket scientist to see that everyone at the table realized it.

Jealousy had Allie's stomach twisted into knots. Jealousy of Hannah's popularity with her new family. Of Hannah liking Bitty so much. Of Bitty liking her. Of Big Joe salivating over Hannah. Of Allie being less popular. Of Allie *never* being popular.

Of being destined to be a loser . . . and all alone again.

Swallowing hard, she glowered at Hannah from across the table and realized how much she both hated and admired the girl's beauty. She had to admit, as much as she didn't like the attention Hannah was getting, it was really difficult to take her eyes off of her. *Just something I'll try not to hate you for*, she thought, staring at her new friend. *And you will never, and I mean NEVER, eat at this table again. Not if I have anything to do with it.*

"I wish I could be homeschooled," Hannah was telling Miss Bitty, her voice practically dripping with honey. "Especially if my house was as nice and cozy as yours, Miss Bitty."

That was another thing that was angering Allie. Dinner had started only fifteen minutes ago and already Hannah had complimented Bitty more times than she could count. Why was she working so hard to kiss up to the old woman?

Even more disgusting, Big Joe was at the end of the table hanging on to every word the girl was saying.

"Well, Allie's in good hands with Louis," Miss Bitty said, smiling at Hannah. "We were fortunate he had the time to tutor her."

Hannah turned to Louis and smiled demurely. "Hey, maybe you can homeschool me, too. I can talk to my stepdad. He might totally go for it."

Like hell he would. Allie's grip on her glass tightened. Louis was *hers*. Miss Bitty was hers. Even Big Joe: HERS.

Yes, they were a motley bunch and certainly not a textbook family, but they were all she had. The only real home and stability she'd ever known—and, if she had to, she would fight tooth and nail to keep them.

"My schedule is pretty full right now," Louis said. "But if you want me to I can give you the names of a couple of colleagues of mine. I'd be happy to."

Hannah's face fell and she poked out a plump lower lip. "Aw, okay."

"So Miss Bitty says you're from California. What part?" Big Joe asked.

Hannah's face brightened. "The Valley."

"Aw, the Valley," Big Joe said, smiling. "I have fond memories of that area. I live in Santa Monica now, but I do business out there sometimes."

"If you live in California, why are you here?"

Big Joe pointed at Miss Bitty. "She's whipping me into shape. I was pretty healthy when I was young, then *this* happened," he said, motioning to his stomach.

"Wow, you came all the way out here to lose weight?"

"They say she's the best. Besides, we go way back."

"We do," Miss Bitty said. "In fact, Louis is from California, too."

Hannah's eyes lit up. "Really? Wow, that's wild! I've probably met more Californians here than Louisianans."

Allie wondered if anyone would notice if she got up and went to her room. *Yeah, probably not,* she thought, clenching her jaw.

Hannah turned back to Miss Bitty. "If you need any help around here, let me know. I'm serious. I want to go into the wellness industry, too, and would love to study under someone like you."

Allie scowled. *Go ahead and pop some pills—and quit acting like such a freaking Girl Scout.*

Bitty smiled. "Thank you, Hannah. I'll be sure to keep that in mind."

Allie's throat was so dry, she couldn't get food down it. She glanced at Louis and caught him studying her. "You okay?" he asked. "You look a little flushed." It was the only time anyone had addressed her during the whole dinner.

Allie glared at him.

Suddenly all eyes were on her. But not in the way she'd hoped. She jumped a little and her foot landed hard on Piglet's tail. The animal yelped.

"Oh, God, sorry," she said, watching the little dog bolt out of the room.

Big Joe, oblivious to Allie's dark mood, turned to her and smiled. "Well, Allie. I'm glad to see you've made such a nice friend here. Hannah seems beautiful both inside and out."

Enough! Allie threw her napkin into her plate. "Really. Could you be more of a *perv*, Joe?" she spat.

The smile slipped off Joe's face.

"Allie!" Miss Bitty scolded.

Chair legs screeched loudly against the hardwood floor as Allie shot up and headed for the living room.

"Where are you going?" Miss Bitty called.

"Some place where I can throw up."

———

Back in her room, Allie lay on her bed and stroked Piglet's small back. She knew she was behaving like a child.

Great, she thought. After all the hard work she'd been doing, she had to make a fool out of herself. The new Allie would've definitely kept her cool. But in all honesty, she only half cared. Her brain wasn't ready to listen to logic.

She was still seeing green.

The door opened and Hannah poked her disgustingly beautiful face inside. "Is everything alright? Did I do something to make you mad?"

Hannah studied Allie's face and concern crept into her eyes. "Oh shit. I guess I did."

CHAPTER 40

THE SKY WAS darkening fast, but his mood was much darker.

Being interrupted during his evening with the brunette had ruined everything. Usually a hunt bought him years before the rage became unmanageable again, but this time both the rage and the itch returned almost immediately.

Hope had been gone for nearly three weeks. And he'd had fewer chances to be alone with the young girl. Since news of the brunette's murder had gotten out, the old woman seemed to always be around, keeping guard.

So despite the risk, he again stood, sweating, outside the supermarket. He knew it was a sloppy move, but he needed some peace. He needed to take action. To do what he *knew* would relieve the pain.

Thankfully, news of the brunette's murder seemed to have blown over after only a couple of weeks. The composite sketch looked much more like a man the woman had recently gone on a couple of dates with . . . and considering the ex had a history of domestic violence and the brunette had just stopped seeing him, he was the sheriff's department's main person of interest in the case.

He couldn't have planned it better himself.

He was so deep in thought, he didn't even notice her until she was about ten feet from him. It startled him when he realized it was her.

Hope. She was back in town and walking toward the supermarket. Seeing him, a look of recognition passed over her face. She smiled. "Hey, don't I know you from somewhere?"

He was so stunned to see her, he couldn't get his tongue to work. Blinking rapidly, he tried to smile, but his muscles wouldn't cooperate.

"I mean, I never forget a face," she continued. She tilted her head and stared, trying to place him.

The muscle in his cheek jumped and his face felt all wrong. Mortified, he tried to say something, but his tongue was too thick.

Her smile vanished. "Oh," she said with a frown. "Never . . . never mind." And she hurried into the supermarket.

Stupid! Stupid! Stupid! he admonished himself as he rushed to get to Hope's house before she did. He tried to shove the memory of the way she'd looked at him into the back of his brain. Her reaction to how moronic he must've looked struggling to smile, struggling to say something to her, but freezing instead. Her arrival had taken him completely off guard and his body had failed him.

He just wanted to forget it all and enjoy a nice, therapeutic, calming night . . . under her bed.

And if that wasn't enough, he'd hunt.

After about fifteen minutes he heard her car drive up. A few minutes after that, she walked into the bedroom, trailing luggage behind her and, again, holding a knife.

His cute but strange little Hope. Never far from her weapon.

But that was okay. He had a knife, too.

He instantly smelled her scent: a mixture of flowers and citrus. He closed his eyes and sighed quietly, careful to stay as still as possible.

She plopped down on the bed and he could hear the sound of her dialing a number on the phone.

"Hey," she said, "I just got in."

Pause.

"No, the trip was fine. But hey, something really creeped me out earlier. I went to the market to pick up a few things and a guy was standing outside. I've seen him before, standing in the exact same spot, and well, something just seemed really weird. Like, I mean, *off* about him. Seriously. The hair is *still* standing on the back of my neck."

He knew he should've gone to a different supermarket, but he had felt so desperate and had just driven there instead. *Sloppy. So very sloppy.* He was very displeased with himself.

"Yeah, I know, right? And there was this odd look on his face."

Pause.

"I'm not sure, but I just got this, I don't know . . . this terrible feeling about him. Like he was disturbed or something."

Disturbed?

Anger rushed through him. Suddenly he felt claustrophobic in the small space under the woman's bed and he had the intense urge to vomit. He clapped his hand over his mouth and tried to stop it.

He tried to control his breathing. He'd waited so long for her to return . . . only for her to humiliate him. For her to turn on him. And he'd even spared her life. He could hardly believe it.

Vomit rose up his throat and he made a gurgling sound. He tensed, ready to fly out from beneath the bed. To—

But she kept babbling about him to her friend on the phone.

Little did she know, but she'd just changed her script. Her act three could have been uneventful. Pleasant even. But not now. No, she was going to pay.

Not tonight.

He felt too sick.

But soon.

A minute later, Hope ended her phone call and went to the bathroom to run a bath.

He slipped out from under the bed and left the house. After vomiting in a neighbor's backyard, he drove aimlessly . . . infuriated and in more need of peace than ever.

CHAPTER 41

"PLEASE? PRETTY PLEASE?" Hannah pled, sprawled out at the foot of Allie's bed, rubbing Piglet's spotted belly. For the last ten minutes, she'd been begging Allie to take her to her childhood house. She said she was just curious about where Allie had grown up, but Allie knew better. Hannah just wanted to see where all the murders had taken place. To Hannah, Allie's childhood house was some type of carnival attraction.

"Please?"

Allie studied her, knowing that the girl probably got a lot of things with that word . . . and those eyes of hers. Allie scowled at Hannah and grabbed Piglet.

Hannah's eyes narrowed and she poked her lower lip out again. "You know, it doesn't seem like you like me very much anymore. Maybe I should just go home."

No, she *did* like Hannah. She just didn't like the attention the girl got, especially on *her* turf. But maybe she should just relax. After all, if she blew this, she'd have zero friends. She was lucky that Hannah was even giving her a chance.

Massaging the space between Piglet's eyes, she tried to make her decision. Not only would she win points with Hannah, sneaking out would serve Miss Bitty right for paying so much attention to Hannah during dinner. For forgetting that Allie even existed. Yeah, maybe it'd just been for fifteen or so minutes, but still.

"Please? Puh-lease?" Hannah whispered, making a really pathetic face.

Allie sighed, knowing good and well she was doing the wrong thing. "Crap. Okay, okay. Fine. I'll take you."

"Yes!"

———

Half past eleven, the light in Miss Bitty's room went out and the girls slipped into the woods.

Carrying the green backpack with Piglet in it, Allie hurriedly led the way. The night was still as they walked, crisp autumn leaves crunching beneath their tennis shoes.

For some reason the woods unnerved her tonight. Maybe because she knew the single mother had been murdered not too far away. But she pushed on and tried not to think about it.

It had become annoyingly obvious that Hannah had planned all along on talking Allie into going. After all, in her overnight bag she'd packed two flashlights whose beams were now trained on the ground ahead of them.

"What happened back there anyway?" Hannah asked.

"What do you mean?"

"At dinner. It was obvious you were pissed. Was it something I did? Seriously, why won't you tell me?"

"Why do you think it had anything to do with you? Did you *do* something that would've pissed me off?" Allie challenged.

A slight pause. Then, "No. Of course not."

In the darkness, Allie narrowed her eyes. *Am I just paranoid or did I just hear something funny in her voice?* "Maybe I'm just tired," Allie lied. "I've had trouble sleeping lately."

"Yeah, I noticed you kind of looked like shit tonight."

Allie's breath hitched. She pointed her beam in the girl's eyes and scowled.

"I'm just kidding!" Hannah said playfully, shielding her eyes. "C'mon. Loosen up. Get the stick out of your ass and relax for once!"

Yeah, sure. I'll get the stick out . . . and I'll jam it in—

The two walked in silence for a couple of minutes.

"I could swear that someone watches me while I sleep," Allie heard herself admit. The urge to talk to someone, *anyone* at this point, about what had been happening to her was overwhelming.

Hannah froze in her tracks.

"I mean, not every night, but there's been a bunch of them— and I have no clue who it is."

"Wha-at? Watching you sleep? You've got to be kidding me." Allie wished she were.

"Seriously, that's, like, really freaky."

"Yeah, I know."

"Wow. What if I get murdered by, like, some ax murderer just because I know you? Because you and I hang out?"

Allie bristled and shone the light directly in the girl's eyes again. "That's not funny."

"Hey, it could happen."

"Yeah and a sinkhole could just appear right now and suck up your insensitive California ass."

Hannah seemed to think about it. "Yeah, but it's probably not as likely."

Hannah stopped and pulled something from her front pocket. A baggy. She plucked a few pills out of it and popped them in her mouth.

A twig snapped somewhere behind them.

Allie spun toward the sound and shined her flashlight but saw nothing but trees.

"What are you doing?" Hannah asked.

"You didn't hear that?"

"Hear what?"

"Nothing. C'mon," Allie said and started walking again . . . this time faster.

"I hope Miss Bitty doesn't worry too much if she finds that we snuck out," Hannah said.

"Whatever. I do what I want," Allie snapped, remembering the whole dinner ordeal. How the old woman had just ignored her. But even as she heard herself say the words, Allie knew she didn't mean them. Although she wanted to spite the old woman for hurting her, she hoped to hell she didn't find out.

She actually wished she was with Miss Bitty right now and not Hannah. Sitting on the opposite end of the couch, watching junk television with a blanket pulled tightly over her. Feeling secure, wanted . . . *safe*.

Not headed to the house of horrors from her past.

Since visiting the house the last time, she had made up her mind. There was nothing left for her there. Her brother was truly gone.

"If you didn't care that she'd find out, why'd we wait until she was asleep?" Hannah challenged.

Allie didn't answer. She didn't have one.

"Well, I wish I had a Miss Bitty," Hannah said dreamily. "You're really lucky."

Yeah, I am.

"Instead, I have an evil Claire."

Yeah. I'm afraid you do.

Allie could smell rain in the air and hoped it would hold off for a couple of hours to give them time to get to the house and back.

For the next fifteen minutes of the walk, Hannah continued to babble, her words flying out of her mouth like they had before when she was high on her cocktail of prescription pills. She talked about books, living in California, her friend who had died texting and driving, about some other stuff Allie didn't listen to at all . . . and then about how annoying it was that her mother and stepfather fought so much.

"How long have they been married?" Allie asked.

"Almost five years. I wish he'd just divorce her ass and take custody of me. Not like a court would ever let *that* happen, though," she sighed.

"So you like him?"

Hannah hesitated, then: "Yeah—why wouldn't I?"

"It was just a question."

"Well, he might not be perfect, but I like him much more than I like my mother. That's for sure."

"Where's your real father?"

"Who the hell knows. He walked out when I was a baby."

Just like my father.

"So why do your mother and Ted fight so much?"

"Because she's a bitch and he's codependent. She doesn't trust him as far as she can throw him and bitches and picks on him all the time. And he just takes it. It makes me so angry. I wish he would just speak up for himself for once."

There was about ten seconds of quiet before Hannah started rambling again. But this time it wasn't about Ted and Claire at all. It was about alligator wrestling. The girl was a kook, but Allie liked that.

It made her feel less odd.

For the rest of the walk Allie tuned the girl out, because with each step, the sensation that she was being watched was growing stronger. Every time she heard a twig snap in the distance, she walked a little faster. Piglet seemed nervous, too. She growled stiffly from her place in the backpack.

Allie was also becoming more nervous about Miss Bitty finding out they'd snuck out. Now that she wasn't so consumed with jealousy, she was thinking much more clearly—and the idea of sneaking out was looking like a truly awful idea. Plus with the storm coming—

". . . and he's too weak to stand up for himself, you know? Watching it really pisses me off . . . ," Hannah was saying, words leaving her mouth at warp speed. She had changed the subject back to Ted and Claire. "But he's a Cancer, so it's just natural that he's going to want to avoid confrontation."

"Huh? He has cancer?"

"No, silly. I mean his sign."

"Sign?"

Hannah stopped walking. "Are you even listening to me?"

"Yeah. I just don't know what you're talking about."

Hannah put a hand on her hip. "Cancers are notorious for wanting to avoid confrontation. You do know that, right?"

"Uh, no."

Hannah sounded incredulous. "You've got to be kidding me. Seriously, don't you people know *anything*?"

Allie felt her face flush. *"You people?"*

"Yeah, you know, Southerners. Bayou folk . . . *country people*," she said, enunciating each syllable slowly, as though Allie needed her to.

Was this girl calling her unintelligent? Stupid even?

"Oh God. I'm sorry. I can't believe I said that," Hannah said. She reached out and tried to hug Allie, but Allie shoved her away.

For one, she was highly insulted. Two, she wasn't totally used to hugging yet.

Suddenly, Hannah's face was so close to hers, she could feel her warm breath. "I like you. I really do. Please don't be mad." Allie heard her grab her tin and open it again. "God. Maybe I took too many pills and it's, like, seriously fucking with my head. I mean, I would never say anything like that. I don't even *think* that way."

Allie backed away from the girl. "Do you even care about all that food crap that you talked to Miss Bitty about?" Allie asked.

"Yeah, I do. Why wouldn't I? Why wouldn't anybody? We eat the shit, so shouldn't we care?"

"So what you're saying is you'd rather kill yourself with pills that make you sound like a total jackass than by eating things that taste good like Hamburger Helper or mashed potato flakes?"

"The pills help me escape for a little while. I need to, some-times . . . or I'll just go crazy."

There was that word again. A word Allie really wanted to just forget.

Allie started walking again, this time much faster. She was prac-tically jogging.

"Hey, wait up for me!" Hannah called.

A few minutes later, the girls emerged from the woods and saw the side of Allie's childhood house in the distance. Allie frowned. It looked as though a light was on inside.

But when she blinked, it was gone.

CHAPTER 42

HANNAH STOPPED SHORT at the front porch, the beam of her flashlight frozen on the splintering stairs.

"Relax. It's just a dead cat," Allie said, a brisk wind blowing strands of hair into her face.

"*Just* a dead cat? Come on, it's kinda disgusting, alright?"

Ignoring the girl, Allie drew a deep breath and pushed past her. When she reached the front door, she turned and saw that Hannah hadn't moved. "Jesus, Hannah. Move your ass or we'll just go back. I didn't want to come here in the first place. Remember?"

Hannah stared at the house, her beam illuminating the gutted window and the graffiti. She wavered on her feet as though she were about to fall.

"Are you okay?" Allie asked, pointing her beam at the girl.

The girl's eyes looked a little vacant for a moment, but she quickly snapped out of it. "Yeah, but stop shining the light in my face. It's giving me a migraine."

A cold raindrop hit Allie's forehead. She looked skyward and one struck the tip of her nose. "Shit," she muttered. "The storm's already here. C'mon. Let's make this fast."

She pushed the front door and it opened with a creak.

"Wait for me!" Hannah hissed, scrambling up the steps.

Once inside, the first thing Allie noticed in the living room was the television. Someone had taken it from her brother's bedroom into the living room, which meant someone had been inside the house since she'd last been there.

She shivered, staring at the television set, memories of watching it with her brother over the years flashing before her eyes. Watching TV with him had always been a strange experience. She used to watch him go pale and grip the sides of the couch when certain images triggered him. Images of scantily clad women. Anything oversexualized on the television screen had seemed to disturb him.

"I can't believe you grew up here," Hannah whispered as the two moved through the living room. Her eyes found the gaping hole in the kitchen floor. "Oh my God. Were there bodies down there?"

"I don't think so."

"Well, someone did if they bothered to dig that huge hole."

Allie went to the back window and watched rain strike the glass.

"It's freaking cold in here," Hannah complained.

Allie noticed it, too. The house was freezing. Suddenly, a chill inched up her spine, crawling to the base of her neck. Trembling, she hugged her body and stood as still as possible. *It could be him reaching out*, she thought, thinking of her brother. *It totally could.*

Or . . . it could be her.

Gooseflesh dimpling her arms, she ran her hands along her neck and upper back, trying to brush off whatever it was.

A noise from the backyard. Laughter.

Piglet whimpered from the backpack. Turning back to the window, Allie peered uneasily into the blackness.

"It's okay, li'l girl. I'll protect you," Allie whispered to the pup. She was still staring out the window when lightning lit up the yard. Someone was standing in the tall grass, staring back at her.

She gasped and dropped to the floor, pressing her body against the wall, trying to make herself as small as possible. Piglet whined louder.

Who the hell was that?

"Oh my God! What? What's wrong?" Hannah asked, instinctively ducking, too.

"Someone's out there," Allie whispered.

"What? You're shitting me!"

"Shh! No, I'm serious."

On her hands and knees, Allie lifted her head just enough to be able to see out. When lightning flashed again, she clearly made out two dark figures, standing about two yards away, staring back at her.

She ducked again, adrenaline shooting through her body. "Oh Jesus! Oh shit! Did you see them?"

"No, but you're scaring the shit out of me, Allie," Hannah said, cowering against the wall. "Let's go. I don't want to be here anymore."

"What? You mean you want to go out *there*?"

"*Stop* scaring me! Please."

"Hannah, did you even look?"

"No. And I'm not going to."

"No, seriously. There are people out there. Just look."

"I'll take your word for it."

"No, please. Look," Allie pleaded. *Because I need to make sure they are really there. You know, that I'm not just losing my mind.*

Reluctantly, Hannah lifted her head alongside Allie's and watched in the darkness. After about a minute, lightning flashed again, but the yard was empty. "I didn't see anything," the girl said, her words an almost unintelligible slur.

Allie frowned. "That's because they aren't there anymore."

"If they're not out there, where'd they go?"

Good question.

A second jolt of adrenaline shot through Allie's body and she raced to the back door. She locked it, then ran to the front of the house and locked that door, too, although she knew there were about a million other ways to get in. If someone wanted to get into the house it would be easy.

"C'mon," she said, grabbing Hannah. She pulled her down the hallway, to her brother's room, then slammed the door behind them.

Pulling the backpack from her back, she scooped out a whining Piglet and crawled into the bed. Sitting with her back pressed against the wall, she pulled the rough blanket to the base of her neck and held Piglet tightly.

Crap! Crap! Why the hell did I let her talk me into this? Am I really that desperate for a friend?

Yes—yes, she was.

Or, at least she *had* been.

Never, ever, EVER again, she told herself. *NEVER will I come back here.*

The wind hissed angrily, shaking the bedroom's little window. Piglet squirmed beneath Allie's grip and jumped to the floor.

"Allie?" Hannah called softly from the corner of the room.

"Yeah?" Allie shined the light on the wall behind Hannah so she could see her face. Hannah was staring at her, her eyes glassy. "What?"

"You know, Claire was right. Maybe you shouldn't, you know—"

"Shouldn't what?"

"Shouldn't trust me."

Allie's breath hitched. "What did you just say?"

Hannah closed her eyes tightly.

"Hannah?"

The girl didn't budge.

Something banged loudly against the window, making Allie jump. Then rain began falling in sheets.

Piglet! "Piglet, where are you?" Allie waved her flashlight beam around the room to find the puppy squatting in the corner opposite Hannah. She was peeing in her brother's room . . . desecrating it even more. Just the thought of it made her feel sick and terribly sad . . . and lonely for her brother. But she couldn't blame the puppy. It had been a while since she'd let her relieve herself.

When Piglet was done, she jumped back onto the bed and climbed back into Allie's arms. She gripped the pup tightly and cursed her decision to come back to the wretched house. *He's not here. There's no way he'd return to this place, even if he could. He was miserable here. If anyone's here, it's her. I was so stupid to come back.*

She turned her attention back to Hannah, needing to find out what she'd meant. But Hannah had fallen into some kind of drug-induced sleep.

For what seemed like hours the storm raged on, until suddenly, as though someone had simply flipped a switch, everything became quiet.

The room instantly took on a different personality as ghostly moonlight spilled through the tiny window and clung to the far walls of the bedroom.

Piglet even relaxed enough to fall asleep and began snoring in Allie's arms. Lulled by the sleeping dog, Allie sat against the wall, holding her and listening for signs of someone in the house with them.

She listened intently . . . until at some point sleep stole her away, too.

CHAPTER 43

MORNING SUNLIGHT SLANTED in the small window.
The warmth of a sun ray licked Allie's eyelids and she climbed
her way out of a sound sleep. Piglet was nudging her arm, wanting
to be taken out to pee. "Okay, okay, one second," Allie groaned.
She opened her eyes and blinked, slowly realizing where she was.

She shot up in bed.

Crap!

Her feet hit the floor and she rushed to Hannah, who still lay
in the corner. She was curled into the fetal position, sleeping deeply.
"Hannah, get up! Hannah! *Get! Up!* We have to go! Now!"

The girl stirred a little.

As she shook the girl awake, Allie caught movement out of the
corner of her eye.

When she looked up, she saw Miss Bitty. The old woman was
standing in the doorway, staring down angrily at her.

———

Miss Bitty didn't say a word to Allie until after they dropped a still
high, barely coherent Hannah off at her house.

The old woman still didn't say anything when she pulled out of the Hanovers' driveway, but her face was red and her lips kept twitching as though she was having a difficult time keeping her words to herself.

Back at the house, she gestured to Allie to take a seat at the table, then went to the refrigerator and poured a glass of wine. After downing it in a few gulps, she poured another, then had a seat opposite Allie.

Allie glanced at the clock on the wall. It was only ten o'clock in the morning.

Why is she drinking so early in the morning?

Is it because of me?

Allie's cheeks burned. She felt awful about her decision to sneak out. She wanted to apologize, but she knew any apology would sound flimsy. She really had no words for what she'd done. No good reason for why she'd done it.

When Miss Bitty spoke, her voice was disturbingly calm. "Do you understand how dangerous that was? Leaving here in the middle of the night and walking through those woods?"

Allie stared down at her lap.

"There's a murderer on the loose. Do you know how stupid that was, Allie? Do you?"

"Yes."

"What you did was incredibly irresponsible. How do I get through that thick, incorrigible head of yours? How do I?" The woman's tone grew sharper. "Look at me when I'm talking to you, young lady. Don't you dare not acknowledge me when I'm talking to you."

Allie looked at her and saw that the woman's eyes glistened with tears.

"Tell me! What is it I have to do? Are you really *that* self-destructive? Do I even have a chance? Tell me. What do I do to get through to you?"

Allie's heart felt heavy. How could she say she had been jealous of the attention Hannah had been getting? That she was immature and stupid and absolutely pathetic. That she hadn't wanted to go to the house but was talked into it because she was so desperate for Hannah to be her friend.

That she'd never had a friend before except for her brother.

That she was really, really sorry . . . Yes, *again*.

Allie loathed who she was. She loathed that apologizing was so hard for her. Her eyes welled up with tears and words she hadn't planned to say came pouring out. "Maybe you expect too much of me. Maybe I can't be who you need me to be."

Miss Bitty's eyes hardened. "Excuses aren't going to cut it, young lady. Not with me."

It wasn't an excuse. She had meant it. The woman was the only one who had ever expected anything out of her—and clearly, she was letting her down.

Bitty stared hard at her. "Look, Allie. Don't make me fail you because I'll probably be the last chance you'll get."

I know.

The old woman exhaled loudly and left the room.

Piglet growled softly in Allie's arms.

"Miss Bitty?" Allie called.

Silence.

This time she called out more loudly. "Miss Bitty?"

The old woman appeared in the doorway again. "Yes? I'm listening."

"You're right . . . and I'm so sorry. I promise I won't do it again."

CHAPTER 44

Great to hear from you, Li'l Bit! I was just thinking about you the other day. How are things? You make it back home yet? Get your pic up on here. Miss seeing your beautiful face!

-Johnny
PS: I canceled the credit card so no worries.

IT FINALLY CAME. A message from Johnny! Tears of joy running down her cheeks, Allie danced around the room while Piglet yipped happily at her feet. She needed to tell someone, and fast . . . or she was going to burst!

She never imagined she'd be the type of girl who would have a friend who she could confide in over a boy. It felt good! Exhilarating even! Her heart smiled all the way to Hannah's house.

"Have fun," Louis said, easing the car to a stop. "Call when you need to be picked up."

"Okay, thanks!" Allie threw the car door open and tried *not* to skip up the porch steps. When she was at the door and about to knock, she heard voices.

"No, honey. If you really need me to fix you dinner in order to feel like a real man, then I want to do it for you."

The voice was Claire's and it was coming through an open kitchen window.

"No, it's okay. Seriously. I'll stop what I was doing to make sure you get it. I'm here for *your* happiness, sweetheart. After all, that's what God put me here for, right?"

The voice that answered was Ted's. "Claire, come on. That's enough. I only asked—"

If the circumstances had been different, Allie would have turned and left, but she was giddy and practically bursting to tell Hannah about the message Johnny had sent.

About Johnny, period.

So she rapped sharply on the door.

The talking in the kitchen stopped and a few seconds later, Claire opened the door. The lady's icy eyes narrowed shrewdly.

"Uh, is Hannah home?" Allie asked, realizing it was the first time she'd seen Claire since she and Miss Bitty had driven home a heavily medicated Hannah. Surely the woman blamed Allie for her daughter's recklessness. But Allie'd been so excited about the message from Johnny, she hadn't even considered it before she'd come.

"Sure, Allie. She's in her room," the woman said, her thin lips easing into a smile. Her icy eyes even seemed to grow warmer. "Just go on in. I'm sure she'd love to see you right now."

"Thanks," Allie said, surprised by the woman's sudden good nature.

Allie hurried to Hannah's room and was just about to knock on the door when she heard Hannah talking inside.

"It was so creepy I literally peed my pants in the first five minutes," she was saying on the other side of the door.

Another girl spoke: "You really saw someone in the yard?"

"I didn't, she did . . . and I thought she was going to lose it. The puppy started going crazy, too, like she sensed something was there."

Allie's pulse quickened. Who was Hannah talking to? And why was she talking about her . . . and that night?

"At first I thought it was you guys messing with us. Seriously. You sure you weren't there?"

"Are you kidding me? There's no way I'd go to the Murder House, especially at night."

Murder House?

Another girl's voice: "And you guys really slept in his bedroom?"

"Yeah. She slept on the bed and I slept on the floor."

"Oh my God, that is *so* freaky. I think I would've died," said Girl #1.

"Yeah. It was pretty insane," Hannah agreed.

"I bet he chopped girls into pieces in that room," said Girl #2. "Probably even raped them."

Allie's throat constricted.

"I honestly didn't think you'd do it," said Girl #2. "You've got some serious balls."

Girl #1: "Yeah, major *cajones*. I know I wouldn't have been able to take that dare."

Blood pounded so loudly in Allie's ears, she could barely see straight. Hannah hadn't wanted to be her friend after all. She was merely trying to score points with girls from school. And she was using her and her brother to do it.

She just wanted to show off by getting the murderer's loser sister to trust her—and take her to where all the murders happened. *And she had succeeded.*

Allie ground her teeth and pushed the door open. The room instantly went silent.

Hannah's jaw dropped, then she quickly looked away.

Allie balled her fists, wanting to punch something. *Something* like Hannah's ridiculously gorgeous face. She stared coldly at the other two teenage girls: a blonde and a brunette. Their mouths were both agape.

The blonde took a step back and Allie recognized her as one of the girls from Sherwood Foods. She'd been wearing a soccer uniform.

Allie's eyes flicked back to Hannah. "And to think I believed that you actually liked me."

Hannah stared at the bed.

"Stay the hell away from me," Allie hissed. She spun on her heels and left the room. In the hallway, she passed a smiling Claire.

"It would be pretty rude of me to tell you I told you so, wouldn't it?" the woman said, her eyes both playful and full of ice.

At the front door, Allie ran into Ted. His forehead creased with concern. "Allie? Is something wrong?"

"Just get out of my way!" she shouted, her voice laced with tears. "All of you just leave me the hell alone!"

CHAPTER 45

ALLIE THREW OPEN the mudroom door, angry tears burning her cheeks. As she crossed the kitchen, she heard Miss Bitty.

"Allie?"

Allie froze in her tracks and looked in the direction the voice had come from. Miss Bitty, Big Joe, Louis, and Ted were all sitting at the kitchen table with cards and poker chips in front of them.

"Did you walk all the way here?" Ted asked, incredulous. "You should've told me. I would've given you a ride."

Allie glared at the man.

"Oh no. She turned on you, didn't she?" Bitty said.

Allie shifted her eyes to the old woman's. "You . . . you knew?"

"Oh girlie. I'm so sorry."

"You knew she was using me and you didn't warn me?"

Bitty's brows knitted together. "It was just a feeling, Allie."

"Well, if you had that kind of *feeling*, then why didn't you warn me?"

"You need to live your own life and make your own mistakes. Just because I had a hunch didn't give me the right to butt in."

"But I was nothing but a sideshow act to her!" Allie yelled, staring directly at Ted. "She was using me to get some other girls to like her. They dared her to become friends with me . . . the *weird* girl. To get me to show her where my brother killed those people!"

Ted's eyes widened. "Allie, that's awful. I had no idea. I just thought you guys had an argument."

The old woman went to the counter and grabbed some tissue. "Oh Allie, I'm so sorry." She tried to hand it to Allie, but she wouldn't accept it. "There will be other friends," Miss Bitty said. "Sometimes certain people just aren't meant to—"

"*Other* friends? Really? Did you really just say that?" Allie spat. "Well, that's easy for you to say. *Everyone* likes you. No one has *ever* liked me! Do you even realize that Hannah was the first real friend I've ever even had?"

Allie's eyes darted to Ted again. He, Louis, and Big Joe were heading out the mudroom door.

Allie turned her attention back to Bitty. "No one even wants to be around me once they get to know me! You were wrong. I *am* ugly! When people are around me long enough, they start seeing an ugly . . . pathetic . . . misfit. The daughter of a crazy whore and the sister of a sick brother who hated woman and liked to—" Warm tears streamed down her cheeks. "But, of course, you have absolutely no idea how that even feels. You're so irritatingly perfect and people love the hell out of you!"

Allie was so angry she didn't care what she did or said. All she cared about was releasing the anger. "Why am I even trying, huh? It's no use. I was stupid to even think that a girl like Hannah would actually like me. I mean, *no one* likes me. No one ever has. I'm just a used-up piece of trash. My own mother didn't even love me. If she had, she would've told me so, at least once." She was outright sobbing now. "But . . . but she knew I didn't deserve it." She swiped at her nose with the back of her hand. "People hate me and you know what? They *should*, because I'm the reason my brother killed himself. It's because I was selfish. I was so mean to him and just kept pushing him because it made *me* feel better! I pushed him until he just lost his shit and killed himself! If it hadn't been for me—"

Allie had no choice but to stop so she could catch her breath. Hiccupping violently, she stared out the window. "I'm exactly what those people in the supermarket said I was," she said. "I'm a piece of shit, and I just have to accept it."

Miss Bitty's voice was calm. "Do you really believe that, Allie?"

"Yes," she sniffed. "And you know what's so crazy? I *knew* it was wrong to trust Hannah. She acted too happy to hang out with me. I mean, who in their right mind would even want to be around me?"

Miss Bitty's voice was tender. "I do."

"Well, then you must be seriously fucked up, lady, because you're the only one."

CHAPTER 46

THE BEDROOM WAS cool and dark when Miss Bitty walked in a few hours later. Allie was wide awake under the covers, holding a snoring Piglet.

"Allie, phone call."

Allie didn't bother opening her swollen eyes. "I'm not here."

"It's Hannah."

"Well, duh. It's not like anyone else has ever called me."

"I think you should take it."

When she didn't make a move to pick up the phone, she heard the old woman lay it on the bedside table. A moment later, the door clicked closed.

Allie sat up and reached for the phone. "What do you want?"

The voice on the other end was small and thin. "I want to tell you what happened. Why I did it."

Allie waited.

"Allie? Are you there?"

"Go on."

Hannah's voice was quiet, almost a whisper. "I met Kayla and Stefanie a couple of weeks before I introduced myself to you. I was lonely and I really wanted friends, but you know how girls can be," she said and paused. "Plus, people find me a little quirky and odd, and I know that . . . so it's usually tough for me to fit in."

Hannah has a hard time fitting in? She WAS quirky and odd, but still.

"Well, Kayla didn't like me at first," Hannah continued, "so I thought for sure I was destined to have no friends here. But then *you* came back to town and everyone started talking. Seriously—it didn't seem like they talked about anything else for, like, a month. It's all they ever even seemed to tweet about."

Tweet?

"So when my mom said she was going to your house to see Miss Bitty I said I wanted to go, too, to see if I'd have the chance to meet you. I was curious about you, but I also wanted to tell the girls I'd met you, you know, so that they'd pay more attention to me. I knew it was such a loser thing to do, but I did it anyway."

The line went quiet.

"Go on."

"Then when I told them you actually came to my house they got more interested in me . . . and seemed to like me more. I joined the soccer team and thought I was getting closer to them. That they were really accepting me. I didn't think I was hurting anyone. I mean, I liked them and I liked you. But then they dared me to go to the Murder House . . ." She paused. "*Your* house. That's what they all call it. They dared me to go there with you and I knew they'd give me a hard time if I didn't." Hannah paused again. "Even though I didn't feel right about asking you to take me there, I did it anyway because I didn't want to lose them. I thought they were my *friends*. That's why I begged you to go even though I knew you didn't want to. And now I'm really sorry."

"Why?"

"Why am I sorry?"

"Yeah."

"Because that night I realized that you would make a better friend than they ever would. You and I are the same in a lot of ways. Kinda screwed up . . . kinda weird . . . and we don't really fit in. Plus, in the back of my mind, I always knew they were using me. And even though I was kinda okay with that at first, I was getting tired of it. I also started to feel like a really mean person because Miss Bitty and Louis and Joe were all so kind to me. It's like they trusted me to be good to you. And I wasn't."

The line went silent.

"I guess I'm a little insecure. I've always been different than the others and sometimes it's hard. I guess I had something to prove to myself, so I tried to prove something to them. But that's not who I want to be. It's not." She paused again. "Look, I don't expect you to forgive me, but I wanted you to know that I'm sorry. Truly, I am."

Long pause.

"Allie?"

"Yeah."

"Well . . . I mean, do you have anything to say?"

"Okay."

"Okay . . . *what?*"

"Just okay. I'm hanging up now."

"Allie, seriously. I'm really sorry."

"Yeah, me, too."

Allie hung up, then pressed "Play" on her brother's CD player. She rubbed Piglet's belly and listened to "Lay, Lady, Lay" on loop as she sat in the dark and thought about the conversation.

As angry as she was, she realized Hannah had sounded genuine. Plus, it really took balls for her to admit what she did—and she hadn't needed to. After all, she already had friends. It wasn't like she was desperate or anything.

But do I even care now?

Yeah . . . yeah, I think I do.

Allie decided she would call her back. If anyone knew how important second chances were, it was Allie.

But she would wait. She would make Hannah suffer a little first.

———

At seven o'clock, Allie wandered out of her bedroom to find Miss Bitty. It was the time of night they usually spent watching junk television together.

Her eyes swollen and her throat thick with tears, she longed to be around the old woman. She needed to be with her and try to make everything okay between them.

As she reached the end of the hall, she saw light from the family room spilling into the hallway. Someone was in the room. When Allie turned the corner, she was relieved to see that it was Miss Bitty—and that she was alone. The old woman looked up at her and patted the couch. "Come, sit."

The woman muted the television.

Allie decided to not give herself time to think. "Look, I'm sorry I yelled," she blurted out. "Also for saying what I did about, you know . . . you being effed up."

Miss Bitty smiled, but her eyes were red and swollen, too. "If I knew she was going to hurt you, I would've said something. I didn't know, Allie. I could tell she was troubled, but that was all I knew. Honestly."

Miss Bitty knew Hannah was troubled? As far as Allie was concerned, Hannah had put on a good show for the old woman.

Too good of a show.

Miss Bitty placed a hand on Allie's shoulder. "And I'm glad you yelled and said the things you said. The way I see it, it was a great therapy session. What you said was honest and healthy, Allie. You let go of a lot of pain."

Yes. A lot. "But how did you know Hannah was troubled?"

Bitty paused. "Well, let's just say that I know things."

"Like what kind of things?"

Miss Bitty gazed at her and Allie noticed that her red-rimmed eyes were also glazed over. She was either drunk or close to it.

"Well, what if I told you that there was something inside of me . . . a sixth sense, if you will . . . that told me you were supposed to come into my life? That I moved here from California just for you? Now, I didn't know exactly when, but I knew that if I came here, our paths would cross and you would need me. That I'd have an important role in your life. Would you believe me?"

Allie nodded. At this point she would believe pretty much anything Miss Bitty told her, glassy-eyed or not.

A shadow crossed the old woman's face. "I don't know everything, though," she muttered and sighed. "That's the problem."

CHAPTER 47

ALLIE BLINKED SLEEP from her swollen eyes. Piglet was growling at the end of bed, her body erect.

She heard a bump in the doorway, then heavy footsteps disappearing down the hall.

What the—?

Piglet shot out of the room, barking.

No! "Piglet!" Allie screamed, swinging her legs out of the bed.

There was a loud clatter in the living room. Piglet's barks became frantic. But once Allie reached the living room, there was no one in sight.

Piglet's barks grew faint, now coming from outside the house. Allie ran through the kitchen to find the door to the mudroom standing wide open.

Her heart hammering in her chest, she stepped out into the chilly air to see the puppy at the mouth of the woods, stubby little tail stiff and ears at attention.

"Piglet, come!" she commanded. "Here, girl! Come, Piglet!"

The dog glanced back at her for a moment as if she wasn't sure what to do, then she let out a high-pitched bark and bounded into the woods.

"Piglet, *no!*"

The little dog's barks grew faint as the distance between them grew.

"Piglet!"

Allie ran across the yard, the hard ground cold against her bare feet, but when she reached the mouth of the woods, she froze. Something told her it would be a bad idea to follow the dog.

"Piglet! *Piglet!*" she cried, hoping the pup would turn around and come jumping into her arms.

Somewhere in the distance, she thought she heard the dog yelp.

Then, she couldn't hear the dog at all.

———

Allie banged on Miss Bitty's bedroom door. "Miss Bitty? Miss Bitty!" But the old woman didn't answer.

She threw the door open. The room smelled stale, and the old woman was lying on her side in the middle of the bed. She looked so small and fragile, it was hard to believe she had such a commanding personality. On the table next to her was a wineglass and two empty bottles of wine.

"Miss Bitty?" she said, trying to keep her voice somewhat calm, although adrenaline was surging through her.

The woman didn't move.

"Miss Bitty!" she said more urgently, tears clouding her vision. *"Miss Bitty!"* she yelled.

The woman turned over and stared at her with bleary eyes. "What . . . what is it?"

"Someone was in the house! I got up to check it out and the mudroom door was wide open and, oh my God, Piglet's in the woods and I think she's hurt. We have to find her!"

Wide awake, Miss Bitty peeled back the covers and jumped out of bed. She grabbed a robe from the back of her closet door. "Stay in here and lock the door."

An image of her childhood dog, Petey, flashed in Allie's head. Of her mother leading the dog into the woods. "I can't. Piglet's in the woods and she's hurt. I have to find her!"

"I'll look for her. Now, stay in here and lock the door," she ordered again, her voice strained. "Do it *now*."

The old woman quickly left the room. And although it was difficult, Allie did as she was told. She paced around the room and obediently waited.

CHAPTER 48

MISS BITTY SEARCHED the house but saw no obvious signs of an intruder. She hurried outside and carefully searched the back of the property.

Nothing.

"Piglet?" she called. "Piglet! Come here, girl! Piglet!"

All she heard was the chirping of crickets.

She walked to the guesthouse and knocked on the door. A moment later Joe answered. "Is everything okay?"

"Were you in the house just now?" she asked.

"No. Why? Is something wrong?"

"Have you seen or heard anything unusual tonight? Someone in the yard maybe?"

Joe shook his head. "No, but I was sleeping pretty deep."

"How about Allie's dog? Have you seen her?"

"No, I haven't. What's going on? Is everything okay?"

Miss Bitty sighed. "I don't know. Allie said she thought she heard someone in the house. When she checked, the door to the mudroom was wide open and the dog ran into the woods. She hasn't come back."

"I'll grab a flashlight and search the house."

"I already did," the old woman said. "But please, see if you can find the dog. Allie's grown really attached to her."

"Will do."

"And Joe? Even if you don't find the dog, call the house if you see anything unusual."

"I will."

Bitty started for the house again when she had another thought. She turned and saw Joe powering on a flashlight. "And one more thing."

"Yeah?"

"Do me a favor and, even after tonight, keep an eye out around here on a regular basis, will you? There's a killer on the loose and I have a young girl inside who I need to protect."

"Yeah, Miss Bitty. Sure thing. I'll keep an eye out."

CHAPTER 49

HE COULDN'T WAIT any longer.

Hope was working two double shifts and wouldn't be home until at least after midnight . . . but midnight was too far away.

His back and stomach were oozing from his handiwork with the fork, and a fever of 102.3 had come on during the night. In the bathroom he removed his shirt and gazed in the mirror at the deep, jagged, angry-looking slices on his stomach. The discharge leaking from them was slightly yellow. Most likely infection. He turned and studied his back. It was a similar canvas of angry, red slashes.

But he still itched.

He wiped his brow and replayed the words Hope had used to describe him on the telephone to her friend. And to think he'd spared several weeks of her life when he could've killed her that very first night.

It had been a huge mistake.

Rage bubbled over inside of him as he remembered how she had stabbed him in the back. But apparently she wasn't the only backstabber.

Killing the young girl would be terribly sloppy, but at this point he didn't care. It would be like killing two birds with one stone.

He'd finally get his release.

And it would also be payback.

———

He twisted the knob on the back door and it opened with ease.

He stepped in and closed it gently behind him. In the distance, he could hear the soft thrums of music. Otherwise, the house was still. He knew the teenager was the only person home . . . and that she would be home alone for hours today.

He wiped at his brow with the back of his hand, then humming softly, he tightened his grip on the knife. He moved slowly through the room, then through the living room, a fine sheen of sweat chilling the back of his neck.

He entered the back hallway and made his way to her bedroom. Peering in, he saw that the room was empty.

He had once liked the girl. At first, she seemed very nice. But he'd now known her long enough to know that she also had a very nasty side.

She liked to hurt people, so she would get hurt, too.

He heard movement in the hallway. Adrenaline poured through him as he lowered his knife to thigh level and casually turned.

The girl appeared in the doorway, holding a mound of wadded-up clothes; her hair was wet as though she'd just showered. Seeing him, she froze and frowned. "What—? Wh-why are you in my room?" she slurred.

He just smiled.

She scrunched up her nose. "And why are you looking at me like that? You're like seriously . . . *seriously* creeping me out."

He kept smiling. The slurring, her dilated pupils—she was high. *Perfect.*

She stepped backward. "Um, seriously, you're freaking me out, okay? Stop it."

He let his eyes trail down to the knife. Her eyes followed and her jaw dropped. She hurled her dirty clothes at him and shot down the hallway. Knife drawn, he thundered after her.

She scrambled into the bathroom and slammed the door.

He reached the door a second too late.

But that was okay—the bathroom was one of the worst rooms she could've chosen. There was no window in the bathroom.

It was a dead end.

He stood, sweating, on the hallway side of the door. "Come on out," he called.

"You have a knife! Why do you have a fucking knife?" she screamed. "Whaa— . . . Seriously, you just made me pee myself. You're scaring the shit out of me!"

A drop of sweat landed in his eye. He wiped it away, then threw his body against the door. It didn't budge.

She screamed.

Blood pounded in his ears.

"Come on out, sweetheart. Let's talk."

"Nooo!" she shouted, the word ending in a sob.

He rammed the door again, this time with his hip.

She screamed even louder.

The house went quiet.

"Look, I'm sorry if I was rude, but please," she begged. "Please stop. I won't say anything about this. About, you know, you being in my room. Having the knife. Doing . . . this . . . this . . . *whatever* you're doing."

Right. I'm sure I can believe you.

"Please. Just stop," she begged. "I swear I won't say a word about this to *anyone*. Please! I swear! I really do!"

"Fine. I believe you," he said gently. "I believe you won't say anything to anyone about this. Look, I must've just lost my head. I had some drinks earlier and things got out of control." He paused and tapped the blade against the door. "I guess I wanted to snoop around your room a little and you caught me off guard. I was embarrassed, that's all. I'm fine now, though, so you can come out."

Silence.

He waited for several seconds to give her time to decide. But she said nothing.

As he suspected, she wasn't going for it. *Smart, smart girl.*

Clenching his jaw, he threw his body against the door again and a sharp pain burst up his side. Cursing under his breath, he stopped to rub it. But then he noticed something: the door was now ajar, and the girl had stopped screaming.

This made him uneasy.

His eyes narrowing, he pushed the door until it was halfway open. The room was still—and for a few moments, he stared into what appeared to be an empty bathroom. He couldn't hear as much as her heartbeat, although he knew it must be pounding.

His was.

Rubbing his sweaty palm against his pants, he readied the knife.

Was she cowering behind the door?

Behind the shower curtain?

In the linen closet?

The answer had to be one of the three. There was no place else. He slammed the door open as hard as he could—and it hit the wall behind it.

Okay, she isn't behind the door . . .

He took a step toward the linen closet. "Come out, come out, wherever you are," he sang.

Silence.

Gripping the doorknob, he threw the closet door open only to find shelves filled with toiletries, a toilet brush, rolls of paper towels, and bathroom cleaner. Otherwise, it was empty.

She's not in the linen closet . . .

He licked his lips and stared at the blue shower curtain. He reached out and it opened with a shriek.

There she sat, in the corner of the bathtub, grasping her little lavender tin. But the expression on her face surprised him. She was grinning ear to ear. Her cheeks were wet, but she looked at him as though she was seeing something comical.

"I'm imagining this, right?" she asked, blinking. "I just took too many pills?"

"No, sweetheart. This is real."

She shook her head. "No, it's not. It . . . it can't be."

He nodded. "Yes, it can."

He reached for her, and the dazed smile slipped off her face.

"Nonononono!" she screamed. "It's not real!"

"Oh, but yesyesyes, it's very real," he smiled. Then he glared at her. "You really should've been nice to her."

CHAPTER 50

MISS BITTY'S BODY was betraying her. She couldn't eat without vomiting, and days ago she'd stopped trying. She couldn't concentrate on anything except the dread that loomed in the pit of her stomach.

Her ears had been ringing all day. One of the many signs that told her something was very wrong. Something was going to happen soon, if it hadn't already, and she was powerless to stop it.

First of all, she didn't know exactly what was going to happen—or when. She just knew that it would be very bad.

She had become afraid for Allie, so she constantly checked on the girl. Most nights she also went as far as to sleep on the hallway floor outside the girl's room.

She had also secretly hired Hannah's stepfather, Ted, to change all the locks on the doors—and she was locking the doors even during the daytime.

She berated herself again for her mistakes. The only refuge she could find from her stress was the alcohol—a substance she'd had a private love-hate relationship with for decades.

She sat in bed with her laptop and logged on to a mental illness board. For years it had been part of her bedtime ritual. She dispensed nutrition and lifestyle advice to those who didn't have access to practitioners like her.

She frowned as she read a post by the mother of a bipolar teen who hadn't taken his meds for three days. He'd been found on the roof of a Southern California apartment complex, threatening to blow the place to smithereens. She was at her wits' end, having no idea what to do.

She read the comments that followed the post. Most were empathetic, from other parents of children with mental illness. One, though, was just plain hateful.

Anonymous wrote: "There's no reason for these sickos to be walking on our streets. They should all be either institutionalized or euthanized."

Her breath caught in her throat and she saw red.

MizBit777 wrote: "Go fuck yourself, IGNORANT asshole!"

She hit "Enter" and slammed the cover to the laptop shut.

Taking a deep breath, she tried to calm her nerves and become Miss Bitty again, the person she'd been for two decades.

The gentle, kind, helpful Miss Bitty.

Her driver's license, birth certificate, and Social Security card said she was Bitty Taylor. But that's not who she'd been just six years ago. No, she'd been someone else entirely, who'd been forced to make a decision no one should ever be faced with.

Standing, she smoothed her shirt, left the room, and went to ask Allie if she wanted to be adopted.

CHAPTER 51

IT WASN'T THE way Bitty had wanted to ask the girl.

She'd wanted to first confide in Allie about her plan. To finally be honest and come clean. But the situation had become too desperate too quickly and she didn't trust the girl enough yet to clue her in.

Revealing too much prematurely could be disastrous because the girl could easily go to the authorities.

In the living room, she found Allie sitting alone on the couch watching an *Everybody Loves Raymond* rerun.

"Hey, girlie," she said, trying to sound lighthearted.

Allie looked up, her eyes shiny.

Bitty grabbed the remote control and lowered the volume. She peered at Allie and smiled. She was about to speak—to pop her big question—but Allie spoke first.

"Hey, can I ask you something?" she asked, her voice shaky.

"Of course. Anything." She laid the remote on the couch and took a seat.

The girl studied her for a moment with her intelligent eyes but then seemed to lose her nerve. Her eyes shifted back to the television. "Never mind," she said. She picked up the remote and began surfing through the channels.

Bitty placed a hand on the girl's shoulder. "No, go on. You can tell me anything."

Allie's eyes welled up with tears, and she punched the button on the remote control harder.

"Anything," Bitty repeated. "I'm here for you. I won't judge."

The girl took a deep breath, then the words barreled out of her mouth. "Do you ever worry about losing your mind? Like, really. Like maybe you're becoming crazy?"

Yes, every single day. "What do you mean? Did something happen?"

"Well—" Allie started, her eyes flitting from Miss Bitty's to the television. She seemed to be trying to put her thoughts into words. Her eyes filled with tears again and she began to tremble. She opened her mouth to speak again, but then her jaw dropped and she clamped her hand over her mouth. "Oh my God!"

Miss Bitty's gaze followed hers.

A breaking news broadcast was on with reporters standing in front of a local home. A home that Miss Bitty quickly recognized as Hannah's.

A caption was splashed across the bottom of the screen:

GRAND TRESPASS TEENAGER SLAIN IN HER HOME

The air was sucked out of Miss Bitty's body. "Oh dear God," she whispered. "What have I done?"

Allie sprang up and stepped closer to the television. She watched quietly, her hand still clamped against her mouth.

The phone rang, startling them both. Miss Bitty's hand trembled as she picked it up.

It was Joe. "Bitty, have you seen the news about Hannah? Is Allie okay?"

CHAPTER 52

BITTY FINALLY MADE her decision . . . by far the most difficult decision of her life. For years, she had allowed certain instincts
to outpower others and she couldn't . . . wouldn't . . . do it anymore.

She wept into a towel in her room, so hard she was unable to
catch her breath. She knew she should be with Allie, helping her
through the loss of her friend and telling her that everything would
be okay.

But it would just be a lie.

Besides, she was having trouble just keeping herself together.
She had used the hallway wall to support her weak knees just so she
could walk from the living room to her bedroom without collaps-
ing, so she knew she'd be no help to the girl.

She'd only scare her more.

She had asked Joe to be with Allie, to talk with her and watch her
closely for the rest of the evening, and he said he'd be happy to help.

She lowered herself to her old knees and prayed. It was one of
two things, for years, she'd been too much of a coward to do—and
she'd do the other soon.

A soothing warmth always flooded her chest when she prayed
to her maker, instantly calming her. That and an unshakable

certainty that He would help her get through whatever struggles she was facing.

It wasn't the case this time. This time there was no warmth. No certainty.

When she was done praying, she vomited. Then, on shaky legs, she went to the mirror. The old woman staring back looked beaten—and, the truth was, she had been. She'd weathered more storms than anyone should ever have to face, but most of it had been by choice . . . the consequences of making the wrong decisions.

But she'd do the right thing now.

And it would all start with drafting a very detailed grocery list.

CHAPTER 53

ALLIE PINCHED HER arm hard to make sure she wasn't having a nightmare.

Wincing, she realized she wasn't. Lying in bed, she stared up at her bedroom ceiling, a million questions running wild in her mind.

She had talked to Hannah only hours before and now she was dead? It reminded her of how quickly her brother had died. One second he'd been there. The next he was gone for good.

The reporter said Hannah had been murdered. Stabbed forty-two times.

Allie shuddered at the thought.

How scared had she been? How much had it hurt? How long had she been conscious? What were her last thoughts?

And . . . why? Who would want to kill Hannah?

Was it the same person who'd killed that single mother? Or had she just been in the wrong place at the wrong time? Or was it more personal than that?

Did it have something to do with me?

Hannah's words in the woods that night echoed in her ears:

Wow. What if I get murdered by, like, some ax murderer just because I know you? Because you and I hang out?

Gooseflesh rose on Allie's arms, and she hugged herself.

Will murder always follow me?

Am I just fooling myself thinking I'll ever be normal?

Tears flooding her eyes, she pulled the comforter up to her neck and tried to breathe.

Her bedroom door eased open. It was Miss Bitty. "Are you okay?"

Swiping at her nose, Allie studied her. She looked tired, ragged, and way too thin. "Yeah, I mean, I guess so."

The old woman shuffled to the bedroom window and checked the locks.

"Are *you* okay?" Allie asked.

"Yes, I'm fine."

I don't believe you.

"Try to get some sleep," Miss Bitty said, crossing to the other side of the room again. The door began to close.

"Miss Bitty?"

"Yes?"

"You sure you're—"

"Get some sleep, Allie," she answered, her voice stern.

The woman closed the door and Allie listened as her soft footsteps disappeared down the hall.

Allie reached out for Piglet, only to realize the puppy wasn't there. She began to sob. She'd spent hours in the woods the following morning looking for Piglet to no avail. She had been a coward not to have gone after her immediately. Her pulse quickened as she realized she hadn't stopped her brother from leaving either.

Death . . . death . . . everywhere.

She sank deeper beneath the sheets. The stability she'd known for the first time in her life was crumbling fast . . . crashing down all around her.

CHAPTER 54

THE NEXT MORNING Ted appeared at the mudroom door. His hair was disheveled, his eyes swollen. Allie watched Miss Bitty walk toward him, her arms wide open.

"Mr. Hanover," the old woman whispered, folding him into a hug. "I am so sorry."

Ted hugged Miss Bitty back. "Thanks."

"How's Claire holding up?"

He released her and cleared his throat. "Not well," he said. "Actually, I have a favor to ask."

"Of course." Miss Bitty gestured toward the table. "Come have a cup of coffee."

Ted walked to the table and nodded in Allie and Big Joe's direction.

"I'm sorry, Ted," Big Joe said. "How awful."

"Thank you."

"Me too," Allie said, her voice thick. She still felt very confused and a little numb. The fact that Hannah was dead still didn't seem real—even with her grieving stepfather sitting just a few feet away.

Bitty returned with a cup of steaming coffee. Allie noticed the woman's hand tremble as she set it down. Miss Bitty's behavior that morning had been more odd than usual. Not only were her eyes bloodshot and bag-ridden, she'd been forgetful all morning. She'd even dropped a plate a few minutes before Ted had arrived.

Ted cleared his throat. "This might sound like a strange request, but with the expenses for the funeral, things are tight for us right now and I know you have the guesthouse, so I was wondering—"

Miss Bitty gestured for Ted to stop talking. "No need to say more. You and Claire can stay in the back bedroom of the guesthouse for as long as you want." She looked up at Big Joe. "Right, Joe? You don't mind if the Hanovers share the guesthouse with you, do you?"

"Of course not. I'd do anything to help."

"Well, that's the thing. Claire won't be staying. It'll just be me," Ted said.

Bitty raised her eyebrows. "Oh?"

"Claire . . . well, she . . ." He wrung his hands together. "She doesn't want to see me right now."

Miss Bitty frowned.

"They haven't released the house back to us because of the investigation, so we rented her a motel room in Truro. But she won't let me stay there," he said, his cheeks flushing. "She's . . . she's paranoid because they've been questioning her about me nonstop. You know, me being the stepfather and all. She won't talk to me. She won't let me in the motel room. And, like I said, we can't afford—"

"Goodness," Bitty said, frowning. "What a mess."

Allie watched Ted. He hadn't made eye contact with her since he'd been there. It was like she wasn't even at the table. She figured it was probably too painful for him to see one of Hannah's friends. It certainly made sense.

Miss Bitty rapped her knuckles against the table. "Then that's that," she said decidedly. "You'll stay in the guesthouse for as long as you need to."

Ted looked relieved. "Thank you, Miss Bitty. I really appreciate this."

"Do they think it's the same person who killed that woman in Truro?" Big Joe asked.

Ted stared at his coffee cup. "I have no idea. They don't tell me anything. They just ask questions."

The mudroom door opened and Louis walked in. Miss Bitty blinked. "Oh, Louis, I'm so very sorry. I forgot to call to tell you that Allie won't be having her lessons today."

"Is she okay?"

"Yes, considering the circumstances. But I do need your help elsewhere if you don't mind."

"Of course." Louis's gaze fell on Ted. His eyes softened. "Hey, buddy, I'm really sorry about—"

"Thanks," Ted mumbled, shifting his coffee mug between his hands.

Louis's eyes traveled from Ted to the old woman. He stared at her. "You okay, Miss Bitty?"

The woman smiled weakly. "Yes, why do you ask?"

"You just look . . . I don't know . . . a little unwell."

"No, I'm fine." She rose and cleared Allie and Big Joe's empty plates. Allie watched her walk back to the kitchen sink, her light linen shirt hanging from her frame. For the first time she realized how incredibly thin the woman had grown.

"So what is it you'd like me to do?" Louis asked.

"Make up the back bedroom in the guesthouse, if you don't mind. Ted's going to be staying here awhile."

CHAPTER 55

IT WAS PITCH-BLACK in Allie's bedroom even though it was only three o'clock in the afternoon.

Since Miss Bitty had canceled all her activities for the day and forbade her to go outside, Allie had snapped her blinds shut and lay down. The problem was, when her eyes were closed all she could hear was blood pounding in her ears.

She was lonely and afraid. She needed to be around someone.

Anyone.

Miss Bitty had changed—and it frightened her. All the woman had done for days was drink, scrub everything in the house, or sleep. And she had barely said a word to Allie. Right now she was holed up in her bedroom.

Something was terribly wrong.

Allie thought of the days when she was working the streets. How she'd sold her body in part for food, but in even larger part so she wouldn't have to be alone. She shivered at the memory, at how her life had once been. Now she was scared of being forced back to it.

Did Miss Bitty blame her for the murders? After all, they didn't start happening until she arrived. Was the old woman thinking of sending her back? Or could Miss Bitty be losing her mind? Just like her mother had? Maybe Allie did that to people. Made them lose their minds. Allie shivered at the thought.

Crawling out of bed, she walked, barefoot, through the hallway. The house was too quiet and had lost a lot of its warmth without Bitty shuffling around, busying herself with her many projects. Even the usually super-soft carpet fibers between her bare toes felt coarser and unfriendly.

She walked into the living room—one of her happy places—only to find it empty and barely lit. Even the television was off.

She wanted badly to talk to Miss Bitty—to figure out what was going on—but the truth was, she was actually a little afraid of the old woman right now, because Miss Bitty, too, had lost her warmth. The ground beneath her had fractured and she was quickly losing her footing.

Feeling tears gathering, Allie headed back to her bedroom.

———

A couple of hours later, Allie heard voices in the front of the house. She sprang out of bed and hurried toward them. When she reached the kitchen, she found Big Joe and Louis sitting at the table, talking.

"Oh good," Louis said. "I was hoping I'd get the chance to talk to you before I left."

Allie's eyes flitted from his to Big Joe's. Both men looked very serious.

It made her knees feel funny.

"Why? What . . . what's going on?"

"It's okay, don't worry," Louis said, picking up on her anxiety. "We're just concerned about Miss Bitty."

Good. I'm not the only one.

"But first, how are you?" Louis asked.

224

Allie shrugged and peered down at the table. "I'm fine, I guess."

"Hearing about Hannah had to have been a shock."

Allie swallowed hard. "Yeah."

The memory of Hannah's perfect face the day they met in the garden, the gorgeous chocolate eyes, the perfect gleaming teeth, flashed through Allie's mind.

Her whole life, she'd only had two friends: her brother and Hannah. *And now they were both dead.*

"Do you want to talk about it?"

Allie shook her head. "No."

"Well, if you change your mind—"

"Thanks, but I'm mostly just really worried about Miss Bitty."

"Us, too," Louis said. "I've noticed a lot of changes in her the last few weeks. We hoped maybe you could help us figure out what's going on."

Allie shrugged. "I . . . yeah, I don't know. But something is really wrong."

A motor sputtered in the yard, then roared to life. Allie peered out the window to see Ted with the lawn mower. "Why's he cutting the lawn? He just cut it a few days ago," she said. "And it's going to rain."

"He can't seem to stay still," Big Joe said. "I think he's just desperate for something to do."

"What a horrible thing to have to deal with," Louis said, watching the man push the lawn mower around the yard.

"Losing a child. Especially one who's been murdered," said Big Joe quietly.

Louis refocused his attention on Allie. "Miss Bitty canceled her clients for the week. And she's not eating. She's also drinking alcohol. It's not like her at all." He took off his glasses and wiped the lenses. "In all the time I've known her, I've never seen her behave like this. It worries me."

"She seems really sad about something," Allie said.

Louis nodded. "Yeah, you're right. I think she is. But what?"

Allie shrugged. "Maybe she blames me."

Louis's forehead creased. "You? For what?"

"For Hannah . . . and maybe even the woman at that supermarket."

"I don't understand."

Allie shrugged. "People just seem to die all around me. It's always happened. Since I was a little girl."

"Oh Allie," Louis said. "Don't even think—"

"I think she expects something to happen to me, too," Allie interrupted, a realization popping into her mind. "I mean, why else would she check on me several times a night? She must think something is going to happen to me," she said softly, more to herself than the others.

Big Joe knitted his brow.

Allie continued. "And when I opened my door this morning I almost tripped on her."

The old woman had been sleeping, curled up in a loose ball, outside her door as though standing guard.

Was it to ensure she wouldn't leave?

Or to stop someone from getting in?

"What do you think she's scared of?" Louis asked.

"I'm not sure," she said, tears filling her eyes. She wiped them away.

Louis opened his arms wide. "Come here."

Allie stepped into his arms and felt them wrap around her.

"This has to be very scary for you," he said. "Just remember I'm here, too. Let me know if I can do anything, okay?"

Allie enjoyed Louis's warmth. It had been a long time since she let a man touch her. She thought she'd never let a man near her again, but it felt nice. *Really nice.* It felt like something she needed.

"I'm here, too," Big Joe said, opening his arms wide as well.

Allie reluctantly left Louis's arms and went to Big Joe. At this point, just about anyone's company was welcome.

Louis sighed and peered out at Ted again. "We need to find out what's going on. I'm sure, between the three of us, we can figure out a way to help—"

"Allie!" Miss Bitty stood in the doorway, her long, wiry, gray hair down around her shoulders. "I was scared to death!" Her eyes were red and swollen, and she was still wearing her robe even though it was close to 4:00 p.m. "I couldn't find you!"

The old woman's gaze jerked to the window and her eyes widened. "Who is that in the yard?" she asked, hurrying to the window and peering out at Ted.

"Ted Hanover," Louis said gently. "You said he could stay in the guesthouse. You remember that, right, Miss Bitty?"

The woman blinked. "Oh . . . right," she mumbled, her voice like sandpaper. "But he should be resting now. Not working. He's just experienced a huge loss. The worst loss anyone could ever imagine," she said, her voice trailing off.

"He can't sit still," Big Joe said.

As though he felt their eyes on him, Ted turned toward the window. He saw them and stared, his expression vacant. Then he focused on the lawn again.

"I offered to drive him to the funeral home," Louis said, "but he told me he wasn't ready to go back. He said something about not being wanted there."

Why would he not be wanted there? Allie wondered. Was Claire really that much of an ice queen, to push him away at a time like this? Obviously, the man was hurting.

Miss Bitty crossed her arms and watched the man push the lawn mower toward the shed. Rain was now coming down in fat droplets. Before long, it would turn into a downpour. "Poor thing.

You would think he'd take a few days off to just mourn," she said quietly.

She turned back to the three at the table. "Well, since you're all here, I should tell you that I'm making a special dinner tomorrow. And I want everyone to be here."

Something in the old woman's tone made bile rush up Allie's throat.

Miss Bitty stepped closer to Allie . . . close enough Allie could smell . . . not wine, but some kind of liquor.

"Sure, Miss Bitty," Big Joe said. "Is there anything I can help with?"

"Maybe we could help cook? Clean? Anything to help lighten your load," Louis said.

"No, Allie and I will take care of it all. Just make sure all of you are here at six o'clock. Someone please invite Mr. Hanover, too. It's important that he comes."

"Sure. I'll tell him," Big Joe said.

"And something else. No men in this house until then. And that includes the both of you," the old woman said, pointing a frail finger at the men. "And you, Allie. I want you to continue to stay inside this house. If you need anything, come to me for it. You understand?"

Allie nodded.

The old woman stared at the men. "Did I make myself clear?"

They both nodded.

Miss Bitty continued to stare at them.

Louis frowned. "Oh. So, are you saying you want us to leave right now?"

"Yes. Right now. *Go.*"

CHAPTER 56

MISS BITTY STARED at her spread: fried pork chops, deep-fried tater tots, collard greens soaked in bacon grease, cherry pie à la mode, pan-fried beignets, a large bowl of SpaghettiOs with franks, a platter of eggs sunny-side up, homemade biscuits, pork sausage gravy, Pop-Tarts, and Franken Berry cereal. Everything neatly arranged on the dining room table.

On the island were six-packs of Coca-Cola and Barq's root beer—the ones that came in little glass bottles.

She clutched herself tightly as everyone—Allie, Joe, Louis, and Ted—sat down, then glanced around, questioningly, at one another. When their eyes met hers, she saw confusion. The tension in the room was so thick it could be sliced with a knife.

Bitty knew that everyone probably thought that she'd lost it. The truth was, she had—but it had happened years ago, and now she was going to make it right. Even if it killed her.

Which it very well might.

Through her pain, she wore a big smile . . . one so big it hurt.

Big Joe was the first to speak. "You okay, Miss Bitty?" he asked.

She pretended not to hear him. Instead, she spoke to the table. "The Franken Berry cereal, well, it was hard to find. Apparently it's now a special edition item," she said, fearing her face would crumple at any moment. "Would anyone like some? Louis? Joe? How about you, Ted?"

"I don't think I should, Miss Bitty," Joe sputtered. "I've been doing so well with—"

"For God's sake, go on. Just eat some! You know you want to," she snapped, her smile straining.

The room went silent.

"Sorry, Joe," she said. "Eating it will be fine. But if you would prefer me to make you a different meal . . ."

"No, Miss Bitty. This looks great," he said, dutifully spooning food onto his plate.

After a while, she saw Joe finally—but hesitantly—break an egg yolk with one of the biscuits. It was clear he wasn't comfortable with the situation, but she also knew that he didn't want to upset her.

She watched Louis chew on a Pop-Tart. Ted ate some of the Franken Berry cereal and sipped coffee. Allie just sat with her arms crossed, frowning.

The old woman tried to strike up some conversation. She wanted them to relax and enjoy their meal. Especially him, the son she hadn't lost once, but twice. First, when he was sixteen and admitted to killing a classmate, and the second time, when he was twenty-three and she had learned he murdered a woman who worked at their local Blockbuster store.

Swallowing hard, she accepted the fact she was about to lose him for a third time . . . the final time.

And this time would be the most painful.

She knew that she had gone overboard with the spread, but she wanted him to be able to eat his favorite foods in peace—and his favorite foods had, by far, always been breakfast foods.

He had never had a shot at lasting happiness. He'd been severely touched with mental illness, an illness that had plagued their family for decades. Miss Bitty's own mother had committed suicide when Bitty was just six years old. Her grandmother had committed suicide when her mother was only ten. And most of the others in their family hadn't fared much better. Whether it was bipolar disorder, paranoid schizophrenia, multiple personality disorder . . . most had suffered with something awful. But, as far as she knew, he was the only one who'd been violent toward others.

He had been her best work, and her worst.

She would never forget the night when it all started. He had arrived home late, his skin ashen. He stumbled in, vomited on the kitchen floor, then admitted what he'd done to one of his classmates.

Listening to him, she started shaking and didn't stop for weeks.

She made him promise not to breathe a word about what he'd done to anyone; then a month later she moved them to a different town. She was doing what she, at the time, figured any good mother would do.

She was protecting her child.

It turned out that no one who saw the teenagers together on the bike path paid close enough attention to him to give an accurate description, so he got off scot-free.

But she didn't.

She glanced at him and noticed he was staring at her now. He looked tense, unsure . . . maybe a little afraid. She smiled at him, the most genuine smile she could muster, and his countenance shifted a little. It seemed to relax him and he smiled back—a relaxed, trusting smile.

He still trusted her. Her insides twisted at the thought.

Her heart tumbled into her stomach . . . and shattered.

CHAPTER 57

WHAT THE FUCK just happened? he wondered as he pulled away from the house and onto the street, needing badly to drive and think.

Dark walls of trees loomed on both sides of the road as he raced down the curving, rural roads trying to figure out what was going on.

Why was SHE acting so odd? So nervous? The way she'd been behaving lately unnerved him. A sense of foreboding bloomed in the pit of his stomach as he thought of the food she'd prepared, of the strange good-bye as he walked out the back door. The lingering, too-tight hug she'd given him, the kisses she planted on his cheeks and forehead.

She also refused to look into his eyes.

Why?

After five minutes of aimless driving, he slammed on the brakes.

She didn't believe him anymore. It's why she'd served his favorite childhood foods at dinner. And why she had become so fiercely protective of the girl. Not because she knew a faceless killer was on the loose.

But because she knew it was him.

The realization jarred him like a blow to the stomach. The moment he had dreaded his entire adult life had finally come. She'd finally realized what he'd been doing . . . and that he'd been lying to her. And she was ready to do something about it.

She was going to turn on him.

Abandon him.

A cold panic washed over him. But what was she going to do? Go to the police?

Surely she wouldn't—

Drawing a jagged breath, he realized he'd finally run out of time. She'd reached her breaking point.

Swallowing hard, he flipped a U-turn and sped to Hope's house.

CHAPTER 58

HOPE PACED AROUND her bedroom. "Damn straight I'm scared!" she said into the phone. "A woman and teenage girl were murdered within just a few miles of me. Hell, I already walk around the house with a knife. I have ever since the rape."

She was raped?

That explained a lot: the scar on her cheek, the knives. Maybe it also explained why he'd been drawn to her. She was wounded, just like him.

"Just knowing someone is out there really freaks me the hell out. I'm coming home."

The springs creaked above him as she sat on the edge of the bed. "Relax? You have to be kidding me. I mean, that has to be the most idiotic, irritating thing anyone can say to someone who is freaking out. Two people are dead!"

A pause.

"No, I know *exactly* what you meant. You want me to relax."

He drew shallow breaths from his place beneath the bed, waiting impatiently for her to get off the phone and draw a bath. He had work to do, and very little time.

He had to take care of Hope; then he had to figure out what to do next. He knew his mother well enough to know she wasn't going to change her mind. When she made a decision, she always stuck with it unless she was given good reason not to. And in his case, there wasn't a good reason.

It had been Hannah's murder that had pushed her over the edge. The only murder she could possibly connect him to. But he'd done it for Allie, couldn't she see? Hannah had turned on her.

He let his mind drift to his time with Hannah. With every thrust of the knife, he had felt the rage drain away. With every strike he felt the fever leave him, the fog in his head lift. Now he felt somewhat normal again.

"I'm *not* being argumentative!" Hope cried above him. "My God! Can you maybe just listen to me for a change and not talk? That might be helpful."

He closed his eyes and tried to push all thoughts of anything but the present aside. To focus on the moment. The bed springs groaned as Hope stood and began pacing again.

He opened his eyes and watched her bare feet as they crossed the carpeted floor. But then he caught something out of the corner of his eye. Something that made gooseflesh rise on his arms. It was a roach and it was standing just a foot away from his hand, its antenna trembling.

"I attract weirdos, Greg. That's what I do," Hope was saying. "And I saw someone really strange twice in front of the grocery store and he looked at me like . . . like, I don't know, I can't explain it. But it was so weird."

The insect took a few steps toward him and his world stopped. A fine layer of sweat rose to the surface of his skin and Hope's voice suddenly sounded miles away.

"And to top it off, I walk in after Aunt Ester's funeral and the house seems different somehow. The air feels strange. It even smells different. And I could swear that someone tidied up while I was gone."

Pause.

"Yes, *of course* I know how crazy that sounds. But you're not supposed to talk, remember? Thank you."

The roach took another step forward. Then, as though it sensed his fear, it moved forward more boldly. "Jesus, get away from me!" he hissed between clenched teeth, vomit rising in his throat.

Hope was still jabbering in her faraway voice. "Not to mention that someone broke in here and cleaned my kitchen a couple of months ago. Remember? So, please. Tell me again that I should relax because, you know, it's really a big fucking help!"

Nausea washed over him in waves. *Get off the fucking phone and run a fucking bath!* he screamed deep inside his head, trying to will Hope to do what he needed her to do.

When the insect started forward again, he couldn't help it—he swatted at it and his back hit the box springs.

The roach changed course, scuttling up the wall next to him. Relieved, he took a deep breath, but then he realized that the room had gone silent.

Hope was no longer talking to her friend.

He could see her feet. They were facing him. And they were very still.

Oh shit.

The woman slowly bent to peer beneath the bed. He lay as still as possible, hoping that somehow she wouldn't see him. That someone would ring the doorbell . . . that maybe a teakettle would go off. Something, *anything*, to distract her from searching beneath the bed. This wasn't the way he wanted to reveal himself. He wanted to do it when she was in the bath. He had planned it all out on the drive.

Tilting her head, she squinted, trying to make out what lay past the gauzy bed skirt. She stared, concentration etched across her forehead.

"Hope? What's going on?" the voice on the other side of the phone line asked.

Sweat carved a jagged path along his spine. He lay like a statue, watching her, readying his muscles to move swiftly.

She straightened a little and took a few tentative steps closer. Reaching out, she used the blade of her knife to lift the bed skirt, then she bent down again.

Her eyes met his and bulged with horror. She let out a squeal of terror. They both scrambled at the same time. Him from under the bed. Her, out of her bedroom and down the stairs.

Blood thudded in his head as he flew down the stairs after her. Once he reached the bottom, his eyes jerked left to right to see which way she'd gone. But everything had gone quiet and Hope was nowhere in sight.

Suddenly there was an intense pressure in his back, followed by an incredible pain. Then a forceful pull and sucking sound.

He screamed and grabbed his back. Whirling around, he found himself face-to-face with her. Her features were clouded with fury and she was holding one of her knives above her head, the blade covered in blood.

His blood.

Woozy, he blinked at her and his own knife dropped from his hand. He stared at her, a red-hot pain blooming in his back. *So this is what it feels like*, he thought, realizing the physical wound was nothing compared to the emotional ones he'd endured.

Her eyes flashing, she brought the knife down again, hard. He barely managed to catch her wrist before the blade sliced into the tender flesh of his chest.

Her palm opened and the knife tumbled to the floor. But before he knew it, she had twisted out of his grasp and shot back up the stairs.

He picked up the knife and started after her, but a muscle spasm seized his back. "Jesus!" he screamed, the pain a thousand times worse than when she'd stabbed him.

He lumbered up the steps one by one, applying pressure to his upper back as best he could with the palm of a hand. An upstairs door slammed and he heard a lock engage.

When he got to the top, he heard movement in her bedroom. He knew he didn't have a lot of time. The woman's friend, having heard her screams, had surely called 9-1-1 by now. He'd have to get out of there and fast. But he'd have to take care of her first.

"Come out, Hope!" he tried to yell, but it only came out as a gurgle. "Don't make this any worse than it has to be," he said, his voice louder this time.

"Stay away from me, you sicko!" she shouted on the other side.

"Come on out and I won't hurt you. I only want to talk."

"My friend already called 9-1-1. Save your sick ass and get the hell out of here!"

Sick ass?

Blood roaring in his ears, he lunged at the door with everything he had, sending it flying open. A white-hot pain shot from his back, deep through his middle. Squeezing his eyes closed, he howled in agony.

His knife drawn, he stepped into the bedroom to find Hope halfway out the window. He flew across the room, and just as she was about to let go of the windowsill, he dropped the knife, grabbed one of her arms, and yanked her inside.

She began screaming at the top of her lungs, so he shoved a hand up against her mouth. Pinning her down with his knees, he managed to shut the window. Then he lay on top of her, needing to catch his breath. Droplets of sweat fell from his forehead into her face, and he could feel her heart hammering beneath him.

Her face crumpled as she pleaded with him. He relaxed his grip on her mouth. "Why? I don't understand! Why me *again*?"

He tightened his grip and tried to figure out how much time he had. Her friend had undoubtedly already called the police just like she said. And then there had been her mind-bending screams at the window and the possibility of a neighbor or passerby having heard.

He needed to do something . . . and quick. The pain in his back had lessened, but he was growing weak from the blood loss.

The woman struggled beneath him, but she was getting noticeably weaker, too. He watched, blinking, as she sank her teeth into his palm. But so much adrenaline was circulating in his blood, he couldn't feel a thing.

He stared at the woman, relishing the chance to finally see her features up close. He took pleasure at seeing her eyes so full of fear. She deserved it after the way she had talked about him.

Bitch.

As he reached for his knife, his back went into another spasm. His body arched without his consent and he screamed. The woman scuttled out from beneath him, jumped to her feet, and started to run.

By the time he got back on his feet and reached the hallway she was already halfway down the staircase. Missing a step, she lost her footing and began tumbling down the remaining stairs. But once she reached the bottom stair, she leapt up and exploded toward the front door and out of the house.

He descended the steps one by one, screaming with each. By the time he reached the front doorway, she was limping in the middle of the street, screaming for help.

He started after her, but froze.

A car was coming around the bend, heading right for her.

Unfuckingbelievable! he thought, his heart hammering so hard, it felt like it was going to explode.

He couldn't believe she was getting away.

CHAPTER 59

AN HOUR HAD passed since dinner ended.

Allie was in her room, still trying to make sense of the evening. The dinner had been disturbing. The food the woman served, the way she had behaved.

Suddenly her bedroom door opened and Miss Bitty appeared. She looked stricken and was alarmingly pale. "Get your shoes and jacket on now. We're going out."

"Where are we going?" Allie asked.

But before she could get all the words out, the woman had disappeared.

A few minutes later, Allie sat in the passenger seat as the old woman flew down dark country roads, the car's suspension groaning in protest as it hit potholes at full speed.

"Miss Bitty, where are we going?" she asked for the second time, staring at the rain battering the windshield.

Silence.

"Miss Bitty? You're . . . you're scaring me."

The woman kept driving.

Allie tried to hold back her tears. Miss Bitty had become her safe place, her everything, but now she was falling apart right in front of her eyes.

CHAPTER 60

BITTY STEPPED INTO the driving rain with the proper change in her hand. Opening her eyes that morning had been a herculean effort. Saying good-bye to her son had been even harder. And walking to the pay phone for the purpose of exposing him was the hardest by far.

She looked around, cold rain beating down on her head, and double-checked that there weren't any security cameras. Satisfied, she slipped the change into the metal slot with trembling old hands and punched in the numbers. She waited for the call to go through, knowing that once she made it, there was no going back. It would impact her and her son forever. Most importantly, though, she tried to remind herself, it would help keep innocent women safe.

Finally her instinct for doing right over wrong was overpowering her maternal instinct—even if barely.

If only someone else would've turned him in. It would've been much easier on her old heart. Now she would have to forever live with the guilt of the women's deaths *and* killing her own son, because she knew he would never let them take him alive.

He was no good indoors for more than a couple of hours at a time and, depending on how he was doing emotionally, sometimes that was even too rough for him. He would get antsy, pacing around. Opening windows.

"9-1-1. What's your emergency?"

The old woman's mind flashed to the little boy who had once been learning how to walk . . . who nursed on her breasts for the first couple of years. She recalled the joy in his innocent little chubby face when he'd see her upon waking.

The trust.

She could almost even smell his warm, milky baby breath.

She remembered all the hours of rocking him to sleep. The first time he told her that he loved her when he was barely nineteen months old. The curiosity in his eyes when shown new things.

He always ran to her when he was hurt or needed to be protected—which is what she thought she'd been doing at first.

Protecting him.

But then she slowly began seeing the truth. She hadn't been protecting him really. She'd been enabling him. She'd been enabling the person she loved the most in the world to do some of the very worst deeds.

No one had ever come even close to him in her heart. Or ever would. But he needed to be stopped . . . for his own good and the safety of others. She only wished that she didn't have to be the one to stop him.

She glanced at the car and saw Allie staring back at her, her eyes as big as saucers. The girl looked terrified.

"9-1-1. Is anyone on the line?"

Wet hair plastering the sides of her face, she tried to get the words out, but they were thin.

"Ma'am, I can't hear you. Please speak louder."

Bitty took a deep breath and spoke up. "I've got information about the murders," she croaked. "I know who the killer is."

For the briefest of moments, Bitty questioned whether she was really doing the right thing. Maybe she had it wrong. Maybe he hadn't committed these murders. After all, nearly anything was possible . . . right?

Maybe if I act fast enough, I can call and warn him. Save him before they get there, she thought suddenly.

But then something bigger than her took over.

"His name is Louis Thibodeaux. He lives in a rental house at 68 Norfolk Street in Grand Trespass. You'd better . . . you'd better come quickly for him," she stammered and hung up the phone.

Not two seconds after walking away from the pay phone, two sheriff's cars sped quietly down Main Street. The reaction seemed surprisingly fast to her.

They were going after him.

After Louis.

"Oh God. What have I done?" she whispered.

Making her way back to the car, Bitty motioned for Allie to move into the driver's seat. Then she sank into the passenger's seat and wept as they headed back to the house.

Her life as she knew it had just come to an end. Everything had just come full circle.

She'd brought her son into this world.

And now she'd taken him out.

CHAPTER 61

LOUIS STARED AT the massive oak, the odor of copper filling his nostrils. The scent of blood.

His blood for once.

Grinding his cigarette out, he sat in the plastic lawn chair, removed his glasses, and ran a small cloth over the lenses. Then he leaned deep into the chair and laced his fingers over his head.

His back immediately spasmed. *"Shit!"* he cried and tumbled to the ground. On his side, he studied the yard and the woods bordering his rental house. Angry rain clouds had gathered over the last hour, bathing everything in ghostly shadows. A storm was on its way and it would be there soon.

As he struggled to stand up, his life flashed quickly through his mind: Stabbing the kid with the pencil in elementary school. Stabbing another kid with scissors. Living a peaceful existence alone with his mother and being homeschooled. Meeting a beautiful, playful young thing named Dariah in the waiting room of a psychiatrist's office, then following her to Louisiana. He knew from the beginning that she suffered from depression, but he had no idea her sickness was as bad as his.

Two months after arriving in Louisiana, they killed two random truck drivers and disposed of the bodies in the pond behind the house. Then, as if by silent agreement, they never breathed a word about the truck drivers or their fantasies again. The hunts had been disappointing, so he decided from there on out to only hunt solo. Also, if he could help it, he would never again hunt men.

Not long after, Dariah became pregnant. First, with a bright but cautious sandy-haired boy. Next, with a breathtakingly beautiful raven-haired girl. When the little girl was just a few months old, Dariah's personality darkened. She was no longer accepting of him . . . the quality he had been most attracted to in the first place. She screamed at him and raged at every little thing imaginable.

He'd wanted so incredibly badly to take a knife to her, to prove to her that he was the more powerful of the two, but he managed to resist the temptation.

He knew the children would need one of their parents. He also knew that he wasn't up for the job. So when the children were still very young he said he was going out for a case of beer but instead went to California, back to his mother.

Through everything, his mother had steadfastly stood by his side, hopeful that if she loved him enough he would never kill again. She loved him so much that she bought into his lies. Then a year ago, she insisted they pick up their lives and move back down to Louisiana so he could finally make things right with his daughter, the only good thing that had ever come from his existence.

His mother had hoped that with the responsibility of raising the girl, he would find some peace. That everything would miraculously come together and be fine. He hoped so, too, but it hadn't exactly worked out how they had wanted it to.

When Allie arrived at the house, he watched her every chance he could get, although he was careful to hide it. He had savored every second he'd gotten with her during their tutoring sessions.

Savored visiting her at night. Marveled at watching her change for the better. He was attracted to her pain. Her life had been a nightmare . . . and he could relate. Yes, she was still very broken, but he was leaving her in the very best hands. His daughter was fixable. He was not.

He had been anxious to tell Allie the truth—that he was her father—a few weeks after she had moved into the house, but his mother didn't think it was time yet. The woman was fiercely protective of him and, in her eyes, his safety came first.

The two didn't know what Allie knew about him and the murders he had committed with her mother . . . or how much the unstable Dariah had told the kids as they were growing up.

And if Allie didn't fully trust him and Bitty—if she wasn't truly loyal to them—there was a good chance she would tell others. So their plan was to not only help her but to also win her trust and loyalty before revealing to her that she wasn't truly an orphan. That they were her family and would be there for her, unconditionally. Always.

The only problem . . . they'd run out of time.

He heard a scraping sound coming from the house.

His hands trembling, he lit another cigarette, then lumbered to the house and opened the back door. Piglet bounded out and yipped at his feet. He watched the small dog as she ran around, sniffing the tree, the leaves, the chair . . . then finally found a place to squat.

There was no way he could have harmed the animal, knowing how Allie felt about her. Instead, he'd only caught her that night and clamped her mouth shut. And since then he had taken good care of her. Several times he had considered returning the dog, but he liked having a little piece of his daughter around.

His cotton shirt was stuck to his flesh, fused to the oozing wounds on both his stomach and back. He pulled at his shirttail and winced. Hope's face flashed through his mind. If the circumstances were different, he'd be furious that she got away. She, like so many others, had let him down. But he was too weak for fury. His brain too numb.

Staring at the tree again, he realized he was looking forward to what he was about to do. Maybe it's why he had become so sloppy, murdering so close to home. Maybe he was exhausted and just needed it all to end.

He wanted to call his mother to tell her he was relieved that his struggle was over, but his cell phone had fallen from his pocket at Hope's house, and he didn't have a landline. He also wanted to tell her good-bye and that he loved her, although he wasn't sure it was true. It was a question that had gone unanswered all of his life. He knew he needed her, so if needing her was the same as loving her, he did love her. But if needing was the same as love, he loved the hunt much, much more . . . than both her and Allie combined.

He removed his eyeglasses and set them on a pile of crisp leaves. Then he pushed his shoes off and placed them neatly beside the glasses.

Lethargic from the blood loss, he tried to climb the tree. After three attempts, he finally made it up to the branch. As the rain began to fall, he reached out for the rope. Woozy, he snatched it and yanked a couple of times to make sure it was sturdy enough to support his weight. Then he waited several seconds . . . for what, he wasn't certain . . . before he slipped his head into it.

His ears pricked as he heard cars approach in the distance. Only an occasional car passed on the sleepy rural road his rental house was on, so he knew who was coming . . . and that they were coming to get him.

His time had finally come.

He looked down to find the pup staring up at him, whining, her head cocked. The sky opened up and rain began falling in sheets. Shivering against the chill, he forced all the air from his lungs and stepped forward into thin air.

As he swayed gently next to the big oak, he was vaguely aware of the dog's mournful howls and the two sheriff's deputies, weapons drawn, running in the rain toward him.

EPILOGUE

Six Months Later . . .

BITTY SITUATED THE last box in the back of the Tahoe. It had taken six months to tie up loose ends with the law, get the adoption finalized, and place the house on the market—and now she couldn't leave town quickly enough.

She needed to be somewhere else to function again.

She had to switch some major gears. After all, everything she'd done for the last few decades was to preserve her son's life. Everything she'd do going forward was to guarantee the girl a new one.

Louis's face flashed in her mind and her knees buckled. She leaned against the Tahoe's frame for support. Since his death, his image muscled its way into her mind several times a day.

The nights were the worst.

In her mind, she lifted a big red "Stop" sign.

STOP!

She raised it higher. *STOP! STOP! STOP!*

Louis's image melted away. A short reprieve from her pain until the next time.

He'd come back.

He always did.

She had a girl to finish raising. One who had come so incredibly far, but needed much more guidance to truly save. If it was the last thing Bitty did, she was determined to do right by the girl. After all, if she did right by Allie, she'd be doing something for Louis. Something he hadn't been able to do for himself.

Thankfully, the law hadn't pieced together her real relationship with Louis—or else she wouldn't have been able to leave town so soon, if at all. The new identities they'd assumed years earlier had again worked in her favor. As far as the law was concerned, all Louis was to her was an employee and a friend.

Bitty still hadn't found the right time to tell Allie the truth: that Louis had been much more than simply Allie's tutor. He'd been her father, and the real reason behind their move to Grand Trespass.

She feared that revealing the truth would cause the fragile girl, who'd admitted that she sometimes saw a monster when she looked into the mirror, to backslide. Plus, Allie was already afraid of losing her mental faculties—so there hadn't been a good time to explain that she had not only one, but two mentally ill parents.

Even worse, two who had literally *been* monsters.

She needed security, safety, love, and comfort. Not more fear and uncertainty.

When Allie confessed that she was hearing—and maybe even seeing—things, it made Bitty's heart ache. She had begun experiencing the same type of things when she, herself, was just a little older than Allie: hearing voices, seeing things others couldn't see. It started when Louis was around two years old.

She was often unable to figure out what was supernatural and what was just a product of an ill mind, but she had learned how to push through it in order to continue caring for her little boy. She learned to be concerned when she absolutely had to be. And to leave well enough alone when she didn't.

After all, only a fine thread separated the spirit world and the physical world, and very few really knew for sure what was real or imagined anyway.

The extent to which Allie's mental faculties would disintegrate, if they even did, would be discovered in due time. But, for now, Bitty's job was to protect her.

She doubted she would ever tell Allie the truth.

After all, what would there be to gain?

Allie had experienced far more terror than most, but odds were, with a lot of love, nurturing, and good, clean living, she would be able to manage. Sadly, these things hadn't worked in the long term for Louis, but Louis had been a special case. One of the tragic few who, with treatment, still couldn't function like the rest. One who had a special appetite for violence.

One who she had just recently begun to fear was capable of killing his own daughter. Until their move to Louisiana, she never would've believed that was possible.

Joe Hicks had successfully completed Bitty's wellness program, and before returning to California he'd given Bitty a lead on a rental house in East Texas, where she and Allie could start all over until they sold the house in Grand Trespass and found something that better suited them.

They were headed for East Texas this morning. Would there be danger ahead? Or peace? Bitty's gut wasn't telling her anything either way. For once, it appeared she would have to wait to find out like everyone else.

The old woman slid into the driver's side and watched as Allie's gray eyes moved over the house. Then Allie got into the car and shut the door. Bitty wondered what she was thinking.

"You okay?" Bitty asked.

"Yeah, I'm fine."

"Good. Ready to start our new adventure?"

Allie fixed her with one of her spellbinding smiles. Smiling freely was something she had only just started doing. "I think I was born ready."

Bitty turned the ignition and threw the Tahoe into reverse. Once they were out of the driveway, she paused in front of the house to look at it one last time because she knew she wouldn't return.

"Mommy?"

Her breath hitched. *Did Allie just call me "Mommy"? That's . . . odd.*

Bitty's eyes flicked to the girl, only to see her staring at the road ahead. "Did you just say something?"

Allie turned to her. "Huh?"

"Didn't you just say something?"

"Uh, no."

"Oh."

Bitty glanced at the road ahead of them and nearly screamed. A five-year-old Louis was standing in the middle of it, watching the SUV.

Her heart froze.

Gathering a deep breath, she eased the vehicle forward. Louis's specter, seeing that she was approaching, stepped to the side of the road and turned to face them.

When the car was directly alongside him, he locked eyes with her. Behind his small eyeglasses, the old woman could see that the skin beneath his big, blue eyes was wet. He was crying.

"Mommy," he mouthed. "Mommy, hold me."

Tears streamed down her cheeks. She wanted badly to stop the car, jump out, and take him in her arms. But she couldn't. It was either keep reliving the past or help the girl secure a future. And she had already decided which it would be.

"Miss Bitty, are you okay?" Allie asked beside her.

Her eyes snapped forward and she jammed her foot against the accelerator, jolting the car forward. Peering into her rearview mirror, she saw Louis standing in the middle of the street again.

Facing them.

Wondering why she was leaving him.

"Miss Bitty, you okay?" Allie asked again.

Bitty cleared the tears from her cheeks with the back of her hand. "Remember when I told you I see things?"

"Yes. Why? Do you see something now?"

"Yes."

"What is it?"

"It's not a what. It's a who. And . . . it's painful. Very painful."

"Who is it?"

"I'll tell you one day," she sniffed. "Just not today."

She felt Allie's hand on her arm. The girl was trying to comfort her. "Okay," Allie said. "But . . . but are you sure you're okay?"

Bitty didn't want to upset the girl so she mustered up a smile. "Yeah. I'm fine."

But she wasn't.

And she doubted she would ever be again.

———

As they merged onto I-20, Allie tried to shake the foreboding feeling in her stomach and concentrate on all the good things that were happening.

As excited as she was to be leaving Grand Trespass, she was even more excited that the adoption had gone through. Miss Bitty was now officially her mother—the only real mother she'd ever had.

She no longer had to deal with visits from her nosy caseworker or Agent Jones's needling, repetitive questions. She was going to have a fresh start in East Texas, in a town where no one knew her.

She'd be able to distance herself from her mother, and hopefully even stop hearing the woman's unbidden voice—if that's what the voice in her ear even was. Miss Bitty had called it post-traumatic stress disorder, but Allie was still uncertain.

Miss Bitty also explained why Allie saw herself in the mirror differently than how others actually saw her. She suffered from body dysmorphic disorder, a condition resulting from her mother's claims that she was ugly, the other unkind ways in which she'd been treated, and some of the bad things she had personally done. But Miss Bitty had given Allie some strategies to help deal with the disorder.

Strategies that were helping . . . even if only a little.

Allie still didn't understand what had happened at the pay phone that night, but she knew that Miss Bitty's story was a lie. And she couldn't begin to wrap her head around the fact that Louis was the one who had killed Hannah.

Louis.

The first person who had made her feel smart.

The one who helped teach her to look at herself in a different, more positive way. The man who she once actually wished had been her father. She still couldn't believe he'd had it in him to kill people. But Allie knew better than anyone that people hid important, and sometimes scary, things about themselves.

No one knew *anyone* very well.

People only saw what others allowed them to see.

She knew that Miss Bitty was having a difficult time getting over what had happened to Louis and that it might be the reason behind why she was still acting odd. It made sense since Miss Bitty and Louis had been very close, but still, Allie was sure there was more to what had happened than what she had been told.

Miss Bitty was a complicated puzzle. One Allie could probably spend a lifetime trying to assemble. For now, she'd work on reassembling herself. She'd let the woman tell her the truth when she was ready.

Earlier that morning Allie had visited her childhood house one last time. It was now little more than a charred foundation. Weeks after Louis's suicide, the house had been torched by locals who believed it harbored evil. And the truth was, it probably did. Too much had happened in the house for it to remain standing.

As Allie stood that morning at the end of the dirt driveway gazing at the remains of the house, she swore she heard someone laughing from the pond in the distance. Thinking about it now sent a shiver up her spine, and it made her even more grateful for having the opportunity to leave Grand Trespass.

What was really awesome was that the town they were moving to was less than two hours from where Johnny lived, and he'd promised to come and visit once they were settled in. She couldn't wait until he saw the changes in her. Surely he wouldn't be embarrassed to introduce her to his family now. Her heart swelled as she thought of being in Johnny's arms again, especially now that she deserved him.

Yeah, maybe she still looked a little strange when she looked in the mirror, but her image of herself was getting better and she was obsessing about it a little less. She also dressed with class now and was a hell of a lot more sure of herself. She was pretty sure Johnny would approve.

Piglet whined from her crate in the backseat. The pup had wandered home the morning after Louis killed himself. Allie had no idea where the dog had been during the weeks she was missing, but it was obvious someone had cared for her. Aside from being muddy, she looked just like she had before she vanished.

Allie glanced at the old woman and noticed that she was white-knuckling the steering wheel—and the tears were still flowing.

Her stomach twisting, Allie looked ahead at the open road again and tried to stay calm.

Life was going to be awesome in Texas.

She was going to have a clean slate.

I told you not to trust her. She's seeing things, the voice whispered in her ear. *She's sick . . . just like the rest of us.*

"Shut. Up," Allie mumbled under her breath, trying desperately to keep it together.

Things are going to be fine, she told herself.

Life is going to change in Texas.

And it was true. Life *was* going to change . . . in ways she could never have imagined.

ACKNOWLEDGMENTS

I want to thank everyone who helped make this book possible: Rhea Harris-Junge, Detective Brad Strawn, Adam Nicolai, Brian Jaynes, Mark Klein, Reida O'Brien, Patricia Bains-Jordan, Travis White, Roger Canaff, and Margy Jaynes.

Finally, an enormous thank you to the many readers of *Never Smile at Strangers* who, after reading it, reached out to me with such kind words. It gave me the encouragement to write this novel and the one that will follow.

I appreciate every single one of you more than I can possibly express.

ABOUT THE AUTHOR

 Since graduating from Old Dominion University with a BS in health sciences and a minor in management, Jennifer Jaynes has made her living as a content manager, webmaster, news publisher, editor, and copywriter.

Her first novel, *Never Smile at Strangers*, quickly found an audience and, in 2014, became a *USA Today* best seller.

When she's not spending time with her twin sons or writing, she loves reading, cooking, studying nutrition, doing CrossFit, and playing poker.

She currently lives in the Dallas area with her husband and twin sons.